MON

APR **0** **3** 2008

TOKENS OF DECEIT

TOKENS OF DECEIT

•

Betty Archer

AVALON BOOKS
NEW YORK

Published by Thomas Bouregy & Co., Inc.
160 Madison Avenue, New York, NY 10016

Library of Congress Cataloging-in-Publication Data

Archer, Betty.
  Tokens of deceit / Betty Archer.
      p.   cm.
  ISBN 978-0-8034-9889-1 (acid-free paper)
  I. Title.

PS3601.R386T65   2008
813'.6--dc22   2007037207

PRINTED IN THE UNITED STATES OF AMERICA
ON ACID-FREE PAPER
BY HADDON CRAFTSMEN, BLOOMSBURG, PENNSYLVANIA

Dedicated to Dr. Charles E. Liddington

Chapter One

It was a gloomy day, a drizzly afternoon in early spring. I was sitting at my desk, watching the rain splash against the rear window when I heard the outside door open. Hesitant footsteps made their way across the foyer.

As I swiveled around to turn on my desk lamp, a man stepped into my open doorway. He stood hunched over, his neck buried inside the upturned collar of a black trench coat; his gray hair disheveled and beaded with rain. He peered around the room, his eyes dark and anxious.

"I'm here to see Jules Ferguson. Is he in?"

As he spoke, he looked directly at me and I had a feeling I'd seen him before. I have a good memory for faces. Names, too, but for a moment both of them eluded me. Then, recollection hit me.

1

"I remember where I saw you," I said. "Richland High, captain of the debate team. You're Dale Lahrman, right?"

He looked me over. I could see his eyes registering the facts as he saw them: long dark hair, mussed but clean, brown oval eyes, smoky lashes, well-endowed T-shirt. He swung his gaze back to my face. A furrow appeared on his brow.

"Are you Andrea's daughter?" he asked.

"Yes, I'm Julie." I knew why he sounded so doubtful. My mother, a former cheerleader for Richland High, had a cute little snub nose. Mine was larger and slightly arched like my father's, which was fine with me. Actually, I preferred it that way.

"I thought so. You look almost the way I remember her. How did you know who I was? We've never met before, have we?"

I pointed to a picture on the wall behind me where Dad had mounted a hundred or so photographs from his past. Lahrman walked past my desk and looked up, his face soft with reminiscence.

"Dad used to tell me about being on the debate team with you. He said you were 'the best debater in the entire Northwest, bar none.' He figured you'd be governor of our state someday."

Lahrman's face grew tense; a muscle jerked at the corner of his mouth. Turning away from the picture, he stepped back to my desk.

"Where's Jules? I need to see him." In the light of

my desk lamp, I could see his skin was an unhealthy shade of yellow and there were deep lines in his face as though he'd lost a great deal of weight.

"Dad died three years ago."

"No!" He shook his head from side to side, squeezing his eyes shut as though he was in pain. "No one told me," he said, his shoulders drooping. "Of course, I guess they wouldn't."

I didn't know what was going on in his mind, but I sensed something heavy was weighing it down. I felt sorry for him. He'd been my dad's friend once. Maybe . . .

"Could I be of any help?"

He lifted his head, a flicker of hope in his eyes. "Who took over for Jules?"

"I did. Do you need an investigator?"

"You? What I have in mind is no job for a girl! Can you give me the name of someone else? Someone your dad worked with? Even a competitor, if he's honest. I need a man I can trust."

"You can trust me," I said, sweetly, resisting the urge to spit the words out through my teeth. "Dad trained me. I know all his methods."

"No . . . no, it wouldn't do."

As he turned toward the doorway, I remembered something Dad used to say: "Always throw a line to a drowning man."

"I could check around," I said. "If you'll just give me a day or two, maybe I can come up with someone.

Do you have a phone number where you can be reached?"

He shook his head. He was standing in the doorway, not moving, just staring down at the floor, giving the impression of a man wrestling with indecision. Finally, he raised his head and peered over at me.

"Jules used to have a safe in the basement."

"It's still there."

"Could you lock up something down there for me?"

"Sure can—if it's not too big. What is it?"

For an answer, he reached under his raincoat and drew out a small oblong parcel wrapped in plastic and bound with postal tape.

"I could handle that," I said, settling back in my chair. He hadn't answered my question and I wasn't about to put something in my safe without knowing what it was.

"It's my gun," he said. "I don't have a permit to carry it around."

I had a feeling there was a lot more to it than that, but decided not to push him for an explanation. Maybe he was telling me the truth . . . but what if he wasn't? What if he was trying to hide a stolen gun? Or stash away a packet of drugs? I didn't want any part of something illegal. Perhaps I'd better look over his parcel very carefully after he left.

I reached under the top drawer of my desk and pulled out the basement key, pushed back my chair and stood up. He looked down at me, but only for the few inches it took for our eyes to meet.

"You're taller than I realized," he said, which I suppose meant he didn't think I was petite and cuddly like my mother, Andrea.

As I stepped away from the desk, he fell in beside me.

"Do you mind if I go down with you?"

"No, come along if you want," I said. After all, he must have seen the safe before or he wouldn't have known where it was. I locked the office behind us and led him out into the foyer.

The foyer was formerly part of the living room of a two-story fieldstone house built years before the US government took over the city of Richland. When the city reverted back to local ownership, Dad bought the house and the vacant lot next to it. I was eight years old at the time, and except for the two years I was away at college and the nine months in Seattle with my ex, I've never lived anywhere else.

The eastern side of the first floor was leased out to a bookshop, and my office occupied the western end. My private living quarters, including a well-equipped exercise room, were on the second floor.

The entry to the basement was at the left end of the foyer. We walked toward it without talking.

I slid the key into the doorknob. "Watch your step," I said as I unlocked the door and pushed it open. "The staircase is steep."

The basement was large and divided into two sections. The right side was partitioned off with thick plywood; a solid wooden door was at the near end. Inside was an efficient fluorescent lighting system, a computer station, a small chemical lab, and a file room worthy of any municipal police station.

On the left was the general storage area with the furnace to the rear. It was always dim and full of shadows down there, even after turning on all the overhead lights, which were nothing more than bare bulbs with a pull string and a metal button attached at the lower end.

The safe was buried in the concrete wall behind the furnace. I led Lahrman back through the storage area and stopped about ten feet away from the furnace.

"Please wait here a minute," I said, pausing under one of the overhead lights. I didn't mind Lahrman coming downstairs with me but I didn't want him peering over my shoulder while I worked the combination.

When the safe clicked open, I stepped aside and motioned to him. He hurried forward, knelt down and laid his parcel on the top shelf, then stepped back. I swung the door shut and twirled the lock.

We went back up to the office. I wrote out a receipt and handed it to him; he thanked me and left.

I watched from the foyer as he slowly walked out to the curb and climbed into an ancient gray sedan. He slumped down behind the steering wheel and sat there motionless as the minutes slowly crawled past.

Finally, he started up the car and drove away.

The instant he was out of sight, I picked up a pair of latex gloves and scooted back down the basement steps.

As I removed the parcel from the safe, I felt certain

Dale had been trying to con me; it didn't seem heavy enough to contain a gun. I squeezed the sides gently. The exterior was soft with a hard inner core.

I unlocked the file room door, reached in and switched on the overhead lights. The whole room lit up. I crossed over to the big worktable in the middle of the room, flipped on one of the high intensity work lights and began to examine the outside of the parcel. It was obvious the entire outer surface of the package had been wiped clean. The black plastic covering was mottled and somewhat brittle as though it might have been been stored in a cold, dry place for a long period of time.

The binding was the transparent postal variety, the kind that has no threads running through it to cause little tell-tale lines when the top layer is separated from the one beneath. The tape appeared to have been peeled off recently and smoothed back into place. A section of it had split apart and been reshaped, leaving a dirty seam about three inches long. I lowered the lamp over it. How strange. . . . The dirty section looked more like soot than ordinary dirt.

With a pair of rubber-tipped forceps, I carefully eased back the tape and laid it out sticky-side up on the flat white surface of the table. I set my forceps aside and unfolded the plastic covering, taking special notice of the way it had been wrapped. Caught in one thick fold was a tiny bit of black residue that fell out onto the white surface. I worked it around with the tip of my finger. Soot. It seemed I'd been right.

Inside the parcel were three articles, each one wrapped separately in a ragged bit of fabric torn from a once white T-shirt.

I picked up the long thin object and uncovered it. Inside was a ballpoint pen, shiny blue with bold black letters running lengthwise: *JORDAN FINANCE COMPANY*. The name was familiar. Jordan Finance was based in Spokane and had branches all over the state of Washington. A lot of rumors were floating around concerning that company, none of them good. Their collection methods were said to be both unhealthy and illegal.

The second packet contained an audio disk, which I temporarily set aside, curious about what was inside the third and heavier one. I laid it down on the table and carefully removed the double layer of cotton fabric.

It was a gun, a lightweight revolver so small it could fit into the palm of man's hand, so dainty it might easily have been intended for a woman's purse. I sniffed it; it hadn't been fired recently. It hadn't been cleaned recently either. I removed the cylinder. Two of its five cartridges were missing.

I grabbed a notepad and jotted down a description, underlining the name of the manufacturer, a foreign company I didn't recognize. After one last scrutiny to be sure I hadn't overlooked anything, I carefully folded the cloth back around the tiny revolver and placed it and the ballpoint pen back inside the plastic wrapping.

I picked up the remaining item, the audio disk, and

snapped it into the file room player. At first, I heard nothing but soft semi-classical music, the canned variety used in restaurants and business waiting rooms. After a minute, maybe two, I could hear voices in the background, mens' voices, but I couldn't make out anything they were saying. I turned up the volume. I caught a word now and then, but nothing that really seemed to hang together. I laid it aside to take to Sam Bellamy. If anyone could enhance it, he could. He was an electronics whiz, along with a lot of other great qualities. Cheerfulness wasn't one of them. In fact, Sam was a bitter man—with good reason. Five years ago, he and his wife had been gunned down at a fast food restaurant by a couple of two-bit hoods that never should have been let out on bail. Eventually, Sam's physical wounds healed; psychologically, he never recovered from the senseless loss of his wife.

I went to the file cabinets and thumbed through the L section, not really expecting to find anything on Dale Lahrman. As far as I knew, after he moved to Walla Walla, he'd lost touch with the people in his hometown.

Patiently, I fingered through the manila folders. La Boyd . . . Lacey . . . Laferty . . . Lagerdorf . . . ah! Lahrman, Dale. I pulled out a slim folder containing some news clippings. They didn't look to be much, just bits and pieces about Lahrman's political career. The last one was captioned: *LAHRMAN WITHDRAWS FROM STATE SENATE RACE.* Next to the caption was a computer code name.

I stepped to the end of the table, switched on the downstairs computer and punched in the code. Dale's file flashed on the screen. For a moment I was too stunned to read anything but the date at the top: October 8, 2002, a date long burned into my memory. Even now, after all these years, I became choked with emotion.

After a moment, I focused on the time: 6:40 A.M. Dad had still been alive when he made that entry. By 10:00 P.M. that evening, he was lying in the morgue.

I scanned the file. The last entry read, "Contact Wyatt Construction Company. Ask for Allen Drukker." Apparently Dad had been doing some work for Dale Lahrman at the time of his death. In all the months since then, Lahrman had never made an attempt to contact this office. So, why now?

Chapter Two

The overhead buzzer sounded, the signal someone had stepped on the sensor outside the door of my office. I locked up the file room and ran upstairs. A short tubby figure in a brown hooded sweatshirt and jogging pants was sitting on the wooden park bench in the foyer. He jumped up when he saw me coming and waved a nine-by-twelve-inch manila envelope above his head.

"I got him!" he cried, his round face beaming. As usual, Gordon Miller had a couple of cameras strapped around his neck. I'd known Gordy since childhood. When I was in the second grade, he and his grandmother moved into one of the government-built houses right next door to ours. Gordy idolized my policeman dad and hung around our house as much as his grandmother would allow him to. Later on, when we moved

11

to the opposite side of town, Gordy jumped on his bicycle whenever he had the chance and came to see us.

By the time Dad quit the police force and set up his investigating service, Gordy had become a topnotch cameraman. He began doing a little surveillance work for Dad and I eventually inherited his services along with the office.

For the past two months, he'd been parked out on the north side of town, watching the house of Roman Gustavo, a man suspected of insurance fraud. So far, no one had been able to pin anything on him that would hold up in court.

I unlocked the office door and switched on the light. "Okay, Gordy, let's see what you have."

He opened up the envelope and pulled out five or six photographs and spread them out on the desk before me.

"I have it on video, too," he said, puffing out his chest and strutting back and forth like a tom turkey in full plumage. Subtlety was not a part of Gordy's makeup. It was easy to see he was waiting for the praise he figured was his due. I made sure I didn't disappoint him.

"Gordy, my friend, you're a genius," I said, picking up first one picture, then another. They comprised a series. The first one showed Gustavo, a weasel-faced man with sloping shoulders and a prominent potbelly, sitting in a wheelchair on a covered deck. The deck was about a foot above ground level and ran lengthwise across the back of a two-story frame house. In the foreground was a weedy expanse of unmown grass surrounded by an eight-foot board fence.

In the second picture, Gustavo's hand was stretched down toward something that appeared to have fallen off the deck and was spread out on the ground just beyond his reach. By the size and shape, I figured it was a magazine of some kind. Gordy leaned over my shoulder and flipped over the picture to the next one, a close-up shot. I'd guessed right; it was a magazine, an X-rated girlie magazine.

In the following picture, Gustavo has his head turned toward the back door of his house, his mouth partially open as though he is calling to someone inside. Then we see him with his wheelchair inched up close to the edge of the deck. Finally, we see him staring surreptitiously back at the house. In the next two shots, he is on his feet, picking up the magazine and returning to his wheel chair.

"Gotcha, buddy!" Gordy yelled.

"Great work, Gordy," I said. "Absolutely sensational." For Gordy, praise was as essential to his existence as peanut butter was to a kid; the more lavishly it was laid on, the better he liked it. "How did you ever manage to take these pictures without being seen?"

He wriggled like a happy puppy. "You know that big maple tree by the fence? For the past ten days, I've been climbing up there and perching on one of the branches that has a clear view of the back yard. This morning, it finally paid off."

We talked together awhile longer. When I thought

he'd had time enough to wind down, I tried to wrap up the conversation without hurting his feelings. With Gordy, I had to be careful. At any hint of a rebuff, he was apt to sulk for a week. I must have said the right things because he let me walk him to the street door, stalling in the foyer only long enough to ask if I had another job lined up for him.

"Nothing definite," I said, "a man came to see me a couple of days ago about getting some evidence on his wife. He suspects she's cheating on him and he's thinking about suing for divorce. I'll let you know what he decides."

"If that doesn't work out, I might need some help on another case, one over in Walla Walla."

He had barely closed the door behind him when the office telephone rang. I ran back to my desk and lifted the receiver.

"Ferguson Investigative Services."

"Are you hungry? I have some batter that's going begging." Nancy Brio, co-owner of the bakeshop next door had long ago discovered one of my sins: a passion for sour dough waffles.

"What's today's specialty?" I asked, listening closely to the tone of her voice as she replied.

"Maple-pecan."

Just as I'd thought; her voice sounded strained. I glanced up at the wall clock: 5:55 P.M. I hadn't realized it was so late. Usually, Nancy was already locked up and on her way home by now.

"I'll be right over," I said, suspecting she had more than gratuitous waffles on her mind.

Nancy and I had been friends since childhood. She was in the third grade and I in the fourth when her aunt, Sadie Brio, bought the building next door. Previously, it had been a dance studio, but Sadie, with the help of her brother-in-law, converted the space into a first-class bakery. Back then, Nancy was a tiny doll-like child with a dimple in each cheek and one in each knee, but after she began hanging around the bakery, filching sweet rolls from her aunt's showcase, she grew into a real little butterball. Later on, she discovered boys and diets.

The rain was still dripping from the eaves as I walked along the railed porch that ran across the front of my building. As I stepped out onto the paved area between the two buildings, I could see Nancy standing behind the beveled glass door of the bakery. She slid back the lock and let me in.

"Hi," she said. "Help yourself to coffee while I start the waffles." As she slipped behind the counter at the rear, I filled a mug with leftover coffee from one of the urns and sat down at one of the small white tables that filled the center of the room. Grouped around each table were ladderback chairs painted either a soft shade of coral or a light sea green, colors taken from the floral printed paper that covered the walls.

Sadie's brother-in-law had installed plate-rails around the room, all of them just high enough to be out of the reach of small children. I gave them a quick scrutiny, curious to see if Nancy or her aunt had added anything new since I'd last been there. If so, my eyes couldn't find it. Every inch of space was crammed with antique china plates, cups and saucers, pewter mugs and bread trays, too cluttered for my taste, but very feminine and charming.

The room was pleasantly warm, the air laced with a sweet yeasty odor that made my mouth water. I sipped my coffee and watched Nancy bustling about behind the counter. She slipped a large mixing bowl into the crook of her left arm and began spooning batter into a pre-heated waffle iron. A big glob of batter escaped from her spoon and slopped down over the side of the waffle iron. She grabbed a wet cloth and swiped at it furiously, then began to sob, tears dripping down her cheeks.

"Nance, forget the waffles," I said. "Let's talk." She nodded and dashed her hands across her cheeks to wipe away the tears, but continued to stare down at the waffle iron until the rising steam had vanished. Lifting the lid, she forked out two crispy-brown waffles and slid them onto plates fresh from the warmer. Carrying them two on an arm, she brought them over to my table along with a bowl of butter and a pitcher of syrup. With a tremulous sigh, she dropped down into the chair across from me.

"Shane's back in town," she said. "Mom called me this afternoon and said he picked up Donny and took him over to his parents' house. Mom said he had a girl with him. She said the girl kept calling Donny a 'little sweetie-pie' and gave him a little stuffed toy horse."

Nancy's chin quivered; a large tear slipped silently down her cheek.

"If Donny's at the Davis', he should be all right," I said, slowly swathing butter over my waffle, trying not to reveal my apprehension. "The Davis' are good people."

"Yesss . . ." Nancy's voice trembled and I knew what she was thinking. It was on my mind, too. Her ex-husband, Shane, had a terrible temper when crossed. About seven months ago, he'd beaten Donny so badly the poor little guy had to be taken to the hospital emergency room. Donny was then only three and a half years old.

Nancy got a restraining order put on Shane, but by that time he'd hitched his horse trailer to the back of his van and headed south to join up with the rodeo circuit. Shane was a bronco rider and a roper, real good at showmanship, but lacking the skill to ever finish in the top money.

Early in his career his parents had financed him. Later on, after he and Nancy were married, she handed over every one of her paychecks to him. She didn't dare not to. Shane could be fast with his fists.

I never could stand the man; he was a phony through and through, but Nancy had been an innocent back then. She fell for his line, and nothing I, or anyone else said could dim the stars in her eyes.

She wasn't the only one. Shane had a big fan section among the women at the fairgrounds. Before every event he was in, he'd swivel his hips around and look up at the stands, slowly parting his lips in one of his white-toothed grins. After he'd captured everyone's attention, he'd tweak the edge of his white cowboy hat with his thumb and forefinger and swing lithely into the saddle. The women loved it.

I picked up the pitcher and dribbled more syrup on my waffle, feeling a bit guilty to be enjoying every bite while Nancy was sitting across from me, toying with her fork.

"Julie, you know what I think? I think he's going to try and take Donny away from me."

"He can't do that! No judge would award him custody."

"No, but I . . . I'm afraid Shane might just up and take him anyway."

"You mean kidnap him?"

"Uh, huh, and then take him out of the country. Mom said he mentioned something about the wide open plains of Australia."

I didn't know what to say. A dumb stunt like that was just the kind of thing Shane might pull, but it would take financing. I couldn't see his parents shelling out that kind of money. For one thing, they didn't have it, and for another, I doubt if they'd approve of any plan that would take him so far away from home. Shane was their only child and absolutely blameless in their eyes.

I took a few more bites of my waffle, taking time to mull over the situation.

"Nance, do you know if he's come into any money lately? Didn't you once tell me he was going to inherit something from his grandfather?"

"Uh-huh. Fifty thousand dollars on his thirtieth birthday."

"Oh, Julie . . ." Her face turned pale. "I'd almost forgotten. He has a birthday coming up." Silently, she counted off on her fingers. "Yes, he'll be thirty years old this coming Tuesday. That must be one of the reasons he came home."

"I think you'd better talk to your lawyer. Maybe he can arrange for Donny to have no unsupervised visits as long as Shane is in town."

"I don't know. I don't think that would stop him from doing anything he wanted to do." She planted her elbow on the table, nervously nibbling on her thumbnail. "I have some money saved up," she said. "How much would it cost to have Shane watched?"

"You mean around the clock? Nancy, you couldn't afford it, although I'd take my shift for free and be glad to do it."

Staring down at my plate, I poked absently at the last bite of waffle on my plate, then laid down my fork. "You say his birthday is next Tuesday? That's five days from now. Why don't you let me think about this overnight? Maybe I can figure a way to find out what he's up to. He may only be trying to scare you. I can't see Shane wanting to take on the care of a four-year-old. It would cramp his style."

"Oh, he doesn't want Donny. He doesn't like little kids. He just wants to get back at me for divorcing him. That's the thing that scares me so much."

Chapter Three

Sam Bellamy answered his phone on the first ring. Though it was nearly 7:00 P.M., he was still in his workshop. I figured that's where he'd be. Sam went home only long enough to sleep and some nights he didn't even do that. He'd bed down on an old army cot in the storage room at the back of his store. There wasn't even a window back there, but it was clean and it was neat. Sam was a fanatic about neatness. Normally, so was I, but if I was wrapped up in an important case I could stand a littler clutter about me without becoming unglued. Sam couldn't.

I asked Sam if he had time for a visitor. Without a second's hesitation he said, "Sure, come on over." As usual, his voice sounded flat, unemotional, but that didn't mean he wouldn't be glad to see me. Long ago

he'd told me if there was ever anything he could do for
me all I had to do was ask. Actually, he didn't owe me
any favors, but he'd never had a chance to cancel a
long-standing debt to my dad and seemed to feel his
obligation automatically passed on to me. Even so, I
tried never to abuse the privilege.

I knocked on the window at the front of the store and
peered inside. A sliver of light was coming through the
doorway of his workshop. The light fanned out as Sam
pulled the door back and came to the front to let me in.
When Sam was tired he tended to limp, favoring the leg
that had been shattered by bullets. He was limping now.

"Julie," he said, formally shaking hands with me as
though I were an honored visitor. "Come on back to the
shop. It'll only take a few minutes to make a copy of
that tape and then I'll get right to work on it." Over the
phone, I'd explained what I wanted. He hadn't asked
any questions then and he didn't ask now.

His store was long and narrow with an aisle running
from front to back. Floor to ceiling shelves lined each
side, all of them neatly stacked with every conceivable
type of top quality electronics equipment. Sam didn't
carry any low-priced goods. He figured if people wanted
junk they could find it in the economy stores.

He was much less rigid about repair jobs, especially if
it meant patching up some little kid's remote-controlled
aircraft or talking robot. Sam had a thing about kids.

"Maybe if they're treated right when they're small,
they'll grow up with the right values," he said.

During the few minutes it took Sam to run off a copy of Lahrman's audio tape, I sat on a stool at one end of his long worktable. A printer for a PC was lying open under the work light. Beside it, a few of Sam's tools were lined up within easy reach of an oblong plastic box, each small section filled with minute repair parts. Also within easy reach was a round juice glass half-filled with a pale amber fluid. Standing behind it, a bourbon bottle held a few inches of liquid in the bottom. Everyone has his own method of coping with pain; that was Sam's.

"Why don't you call me in the morning?" he said, handing the original of the tape back to me. "If I come up with anything, you can come over and listen to it."

He was politely dismissing me, but I knew Sam well enough not to take offense. I left him to his work—and his bottle—and let myself out.

I climbed into my jeep and headed home. I was anxious to get Lahrman's copy of the tape back into the vault, not because I was afraid he'd find out I'd been snooping, but because I'd feel safer having it hidden away until I knew if it had anything important to tell me.

I parked on the blacktop in front of my building. Originally, that area had been green and lush with grass and shrubs, but as the traffic in our area became heavier, Dad needed the space for off-street parking for his clients. Now, the only thing left of the former greenery was a thin line of evergreen shrubs in front of the porch railing.

The light in the entryway was on. I left it burning most of the time; it seemed more welcoming that way, especially after dusk. Almost like a smiling friend waiting to greet me, but a lot less demanding.

After I returned the tape to the safe, I climbed the stairs to the upper story. Feeling restless, I walked over to the door of Dad's bedroom, stood outside it with my hand on the knob, changed my mind and stepped across the hall to the exercise room. I switched on the treadmill and began to walk, a mindless activity that clears the brain cells and allows them to free float.

For the present, I couldn't do anything about Lahrman, even though I had a hunch he'd involved my dad in something unsavory, something that had been left unfinished. A trip to Walla Walla seemed indicated, but that would have to wait. Before I could look into that angle, I needed to know if Sam had been able to pick up anything useful on that tape. I increased the speed on the treadmill, trying to clear my mind of the current problems. When my pulse began to race rapidly and moisture beaded my brow, I slowed the machine and stepped off.

It was now 8:00 P.M. Before I could change my mind, I picked up the telephone and called Lee Thompkins, a TV newsman with whom I had an on-again, off-again relationship. At the present, he was on the top of my list.

"How does a pepperoni pizza sound?" I asked. "My treat."

"When and where?"

"The Mexicana. Half an hour."

He was holding the receiver so close to his mouth I could hear him breathing. After a second or two he asked, "Is this work related?"

"Might be."

"Anything in it for me?"

"My good company."

He laughed. "You're on."

I took a quick shower, pulled on a blue knitted shirt, fresh jeans and matching jacket, then hopped into my jeep and headed out on Jadwin until I hit Van Giesen Avenue. I turned left and followed the road across the Yakima River Bridge into West Richland.

I found a parking slot on the left side of the restaurant and glanced around at the cars. The place was crowded; it usually was. Over the years it had become one of the area's favorite hangouts for the young, and the young at heart.

I didn't see the vehicle I was looking for, but possibly it was parked at the rear of the building. I was well acquainted with the habits of the man I was hoping to see and felt certain if he wasn't here now, he'd show up later on.

Inside, the place was packed with its usual noisy, fun-loving patrons. I heard a whistle and spotted Lee at a back table near the right hand wall. I waved my hand at him, but stood by the door a minute longer, canvassing the crowd. I saw a few familiar faces, but not the one I was interested in.

I threaded my way back to Lee. Two glasses were sitting on the table, one filled to the brim, the other half empty. Lee had started without me, but I didn't mind. The traffic had been heavy and I was probably a few minutes late. As I approached the table, he stood up and pulled out a chair for me.

"You owe me," he said, grinning lopsidedly.

Lee was tall, handsome in a gangly-kind of way and good natured most of the time. One of the things I liked about Lee was he made no attempt to hide the bald spot on top of his head with creative combing. Men who tried to plaster a few pitiful strands of hair across their domes gave me a pain.

"Have you already ordered the pizza?" I asked, sitting down beside him.

"Sure did, a couple of minutes ago." He shoved a basket of chips and a pot of salsa in front of me, then dipped his head down level with mine. "Who or what are we looking for?"

"Do you remember Shane Davis? He used to hang out here?"

"Shane Davis? The so-called rodeo star? Yeah, I remember Shane, lots of charm and no substance. What do you want with him?"

"He's trying to make trouble for his ex-wife. I'd like to help her out if I can."

He cocked his head on one side and gave me his lopsided grin. "Don't tell me you enticed me out here because that cretin is late with his child support . . . not that I'm complaining," he said, patting me on the thigh.

I brushed his hand off. "Behave, or I'll send you home." I dipped one of the chips into the salsa and bit off the gooey end of it. "It has nothing to do with child support," I said, dipping the clean end of my chip back into the salsa. "I wish it were that simple."

He nodded absently and peered out over the top of my head. He laid a cautioning hand on my wrist. "Don't look up. The man in question just walked in with a gorgeous young babe." Despite his warning, I turned and gawked.

It was Shane all right, complete with his tall white hat and flashy western-style shirt. The girl with him was an eye-catcher, about five-and-a half feet tall with long blond hair that glistened under the overhead lights. She was wearing a pink silk shirt open at the throat; a small gold locket dangled from her neck. Molded to her slim hips were matching pink jeans tucked into white knee-high boots.

Whistles of appreciation sprang up around her, which seemed to please Shane. He favored his audience with one of his smug white-toothed grins and ostentatiously clamped one of his sun-tanned hands around the girl's upper arm. He steered her through the crowd and over to a round wooden table occupied by three men, all locals whom I knew by sight. One of them jumped up and grabbed a couple of empty chairs from a nearby table. When they were all seated, I could see only the top half of Shane's head, a portion of his left arm and a spot of pink by his elbow.

I shifted my chair, trying to get a better view of him and his companion, but the wide shoulders of a tall burly man were blocking the way.

Our order was called. Lee immediately pushed back his chair, motioning to me to sit tight while he went to the counter to pick it up.

He returned to the table with a steaming pan of pizza, heaped with pepperoni, olives, mushrooms and extra cheese. Lee always ordered double portions of the toppings. That's the way he liked it, and so did I. That was one subject on which we were in total agreement.

I kept an eye on Shane's table. At first I caught only brief glimpses of him and nothing of the girl. Lee and I had almost finished our pizza when the burly man at the next table stood up. As he walked away, I had a clear view of Shane. The girl in pink was sitting on his lap with her arm curled around his neck, but he didn't seem to be paying much attention to her. He was leaning back in his chair, talking to the man beside him. At frequent intervals, he lifted a bottle of beer to his lips and then offered the girl a sip.

At last came the chance I'd been waiting for. The girl crawled off his lap and headed back toward the ladies' room. I waited until Shane was again engrossed in conversation with his buddies, then leaned closer to Lee and spoke softly.

"I'm going to the ladies' room."

He dipped his head knowingly and gave me a thumbs-up with his right hand.

When I stepped inside the doorway, the girl was standing in front of the mirror, pulling at the front of her shirt. It looked as though she was trying to stretch the fabric to loosen it.

"Great outfit," I said, coming up behind her. She raised her head, meeting my eyes in the mirror.

"You don't think it's too tight?"

"No, not at all."

"That's what my fiance told me, but I don't know . . ." She twisted sideways and studied her reflection, a frown wrinkling the unblemished skin on her forehead. From the view from my table, I'd thought she was a teenager. Up close she appeared to be in her early twenties, but still much too young to be hooked up with a man like Shane.

"With your great figure, I bet you've never been pregnant," I said, making a pretense of washing my hands in the bowl beside her. "It can sure ruin a girl's waistline." I knew I was pushing my luck, but decided it might be my only chance to talk to her. Besides, the soft glazed look on her face told me she'd sipped a bit too much of Shane's beer and might have her guard down.

Tears formed in her eyes. I hadn't expected that. Maybe she'd had more to drink than I'd realized.

"I can't ever have any kids," she said, dabbing at her eyes with the edge of a rough paper towel.

I pulled a tissue from my handbag and offered it to her. "I'm sorry. I didn't mean to upset you." The sincerity in my voice must have registered because she gave me a wan, but friendly, smile.

"That's okay. You couldn't know," she said, her lower lip trembling. "My doctor told me maybe someday I could adopt. And maybe I will. I adore little children."

She didn't look like the motherly type to me. I wondered if Shane was aware of this side of her. I was so preoccupied with my thoughts I almost missed her next remark.

"Maybe I won't ever have to . . . adopt a baby, I mean. My fiancé has an adorable little boy and I think he likes me."

Before I had a chance to reply, a woman opened the door and looked in.

"Are you two going to stay in there all night?"

"Just leaving." I said. I held the door open for the girl and followed her out. "What's your name?" I asked. "It would be nice if we could get together for coffee sometime."

"Holly . . . Holly Raymond. What's yours?"

"Andrea," I said quickly, hoping if she mentioned me to Shane, he wouldn't remember my middle name.

"It sure was nice talking to you, Andrea. I never really had a girlfriend to talk to before. It was really nice," she said again. "I don't think I could have coffee, though. We're only going to be visiting his parents for a few days while Shane takes care of some business and then we're leaving town."

She glanced across the room toward Shane's table "I'd better get back," she said, giving a trembly sigh. "It sure was nice to meet you."

I let her walk ahead of me, hoping Shane wouldn't catch sight of me if he happened to be gazing in our direction.

Lee looked up as I came back to the table. "Find out anything?"

"Enough to worry me some." I stood by my chair, studying the tiny remnants left in the pizza pan. "Shall we leave? Or would you like to finish the rest of the pizza first?" For an answer, he pushed back his chair and stood up.

As we walked out the exit and started across the parking lot, I filled Lee in on the conversation I had with Holly.

"She claims to be Shane's fiancee and says they are leaving town as soon as Shane takes care of some business." I paused a moment then told him the rest.

"Nancy is worried Shane is planing to take Donny away from her."

"She has custody, doesn't she?" Lee said. "Then she has nothing to worry about. No judge in his right mind would hand that little boy over to a saddle bum like Shane."

As we walked toward my jeep, Lee tucked his hand under my elbow and peered down at me.

"I'll follow you home," he said, "And see you to your door."

"Thanks, Lee, but I'm a big girl now. I can make it on my own."

"How about following me home, then? It's been a long time since anyone tucked me into bed."

"Sorry, pal. Another time. I have a big day tomorrow."

"I never forget a rain check," he said, flashing his lop-sided grin. He walked me to my car, patted me on the shoulder and turned back to where he'd parked his van. He followed me out of the parking lot, across the Yakima River Bridge and on toward Richland. At the bypass highway, he honked his horn twice and made a right turn toward Kennewick. I waited for the traffic light to change then drove across the intersection into Richland.

When I arrived home, I stepped into the office to check my answering machine before I went upstairs. There were two messages. The first one was from Sam Bellamy.

"Julie? Would you like stop by in the morning? I have something for you."

The other message was a cryptic statement from Dale Lahrman.

"I'll be in to pick up my package tomorrow." That was all. No mention of what time he had in mind, no telephone number where he could be reached, not even a polite, "Thank you."

The man was really starting to irritate me. He didn't know it yet, but I wasn't about to hand over his package until the two of us had a nice little chat together. What-ever his problem, if it had anything to do with Dad's death, I wanted to know about it.

Chapter Four

Lying curled up on my bed, I wondered what Sam had discovered on Lahrman's tape. If I'd been home when he called, he might have invited me to come right over to his shop instead of making me wait until morning.

I tossed restlessly for an hour or so, punching up the feathers in my pillow every time I turned over. Finally, I gave up and swung my legs over the side of the bed. I walked down the hall to the big front bedroom, opened the door and flipped up the bottom switch on the light panel. The top switch works the ceiling light; the one below turns on the marble-based floor lamp that stands beside an old brown leather chair and matching ottoman. The big square room still had the nice relaxed look dad had implanted on it, much more pleasing than

32

the fussy ruffles and chintz that he'd had to live with when my mother shared the space with him.

The day she walked out on us, my mother said she would send for her possessions, just the furniture and accessories of course, not Dad nor me. Dad was patient. He waited until she had climbed into the taxicab before he picked up the telephone and called Goodwill.

After our living quarters had been emptied of the furnishings and bric-a-brac, he began lugging up the old furniture stored in the basement. The first piece to come up was his leather chair, the next thing was my grandmother's four-poster bed.

During my grade school years, and even after I was in high school, I spent hours at a time on that bed, talking with Dad as he sat stretched out in his chair, a neglected book open on his lap. I wish I'd inherited more of his patience. He never seemed to mind when I intruded on his privacy even though it might have been for the most trivial of questions.

The year I was twelve, Dad accepted an out-of-town assignment and arranged for me to stay with the Brio family while he was gone. When he told me of his plans, I sulked all day, hoping he'd either take me along with him or let me stay home by myself.

That night, I perched at the bottom end of the four-poster bed to watch him pack his traveling case. He walked briskly back and forth from the bureau to the bed, whistling softly through his teeth as he laid out his clothes and checked over his shaving kit.

Now and then, I let out a long sigh, my face as gloomy as I knew how to make it. Finally, upset at his failure to notice my despair, I decided to make one last plea.

"But, Dad, I'm nearly thirteen years old. I don't need a babysitter."

He dropped a few pairs of socks on the bed and swung around to look at me, the green glints in his hazel eyes shining with concealed laughter.

"Babysitter? Is that what you think? Why, honey, I thought you'd welcome a chance to spend a few nights with Nancy . . .

"Besides, it'll give you a break from the job while I'm gone."

"What job?"

"Why, the agency, of course. I'm putting you in full charge. Of course, if you don't think you can handle it, I suppose I can find some else, but . . ."

"I can handle it, Dad!" I jumped off the bed, snatched up a pair of his socks, rolled it into a tight ball and poked it into a corner of his travel-case. "You won't have to worry about a thing," I said, picking up another pair of his socks. "I'll write down all the messages and sort the mail and . . ."

By the time he hugged me goodbye, I was so puffed up with my own self-importance I was almost eager to have him go. The entire time he was away, if I wasn't at school or sleeping at the Brios, I was in the office, sitting in his chair, attending to business. I completely overlooked the fact that although I supposedly was 'all on my own,' Sadie Brio was keeping an eye on me from the bakery next door. It was a long time before I realized how Dad had outmaneuvered me.

A squeal of brakes on the street below jolted me back to the present. I stepped over to one of the windows and pulled aside the drapery. Two souped-up cars, both of ancient vintage, were drawn up side by side, their hoods pointed in opposite directions, the teenage drivers hanging out the windows yelling at each other. The radios on both cars were blasting out a steady stream of rock, the bass turned up so high the steady thump, thump, thump reverberated along the street. Occasionally, one of the drivers revved-up his engine and the other immediately followed suit.

A third car came racing down the street. The driver careened around the other two, beating hedonistically on his horn. With a screech of rubber, the remaining two drivers roared off in opposite directions.

Just some high school kids living it up on a Friday night. Somehow, it didn't seem like such great fun anymore.

Turning from the window, I glanced across the room and broke into laughter. On the opposite wall, two somber brown eyes were staring down at me. Dad and his wry sense of humor. He claimed the deer head with its full rack of moldering antlers reminded him of my mother: big brown eyes and lots of pointed horns.

I closed the door and walked back down the hallway to my bedroom. I must have fallen asleep immediately because the next sound I heard was Sadie Brio's station wagon clattering down the street. The muffler was loose and rattled every time she hit a bump or a pothole. Supposedly, one of her nephews had wired it back into place for her, but it didn't sound as though he'd done a very good job.

The thought of Sadie bustling around next door, preparing the first pans of bread for the ovens, made me hungry. I walked into the kitchen, heaped a bowl with corn flakes, added milk and a sliced banana and carried it over to the window. It was still dark outside, the nearest street lamp casting a hazy gleam on the blacktop. Not a single car passed by the whole time I was sitting there.

I was now wide-awake and restless, but it was too early to go pounding on Sam's door. I rinsed my cereal bowl and spoon, slipped them into the dishwasher and went downstairs to the office.

After checking my answering machine—no new messages—I turned on my computer, typed up the report on Roman Gustavo to send to the claims adjuster, enclosed copies of Gordy's photos, added a personal note—the adjuster was an old friend of mine—and sealed the envelope. I made out checks for my telephone and electricity bills, ran off a copy of a statement for a delinquent client, stamped all the envelopes and carried them outside to the mailbox.

Despite working off some of my nervous energy, a quick glance at my wristwatch told me it was only 6:45

A.M. Much too early to go calling, but I was too keyed up to sit calmly in my office, waiting for a more proper time. I jumped into my jeep, drove slowly through town, circled back and pulled up in front of Sam's shop, intending to sit there and wait until the inside lights went on. I had barely switched off the engine before Sam stuck his head out the doorway and motioned me in.

He didn't waste any time on formalities, but led me straight back to his workshop and started the tape. At the beginning there was nothing except the background music I'd heard before. After a bit, I began to hear two men talking with one another. Sam had done a magnificent job of bringing out their voices, one low-pitched and hesitant, the other strident with a faint nasal quality.

From their conversation it became apparent they were in a hotel dining room, having lunch. They were interrupted by a third person, a waitress with a pleasant, youthful-sounding voice. After she'd refilled their coffee cups, there was nothing but the gentle clink of china and a few noncommittal words, followed by a long lapse when no one said anything.

The soft, canned music continued on in the background, broken once by a woman's peal of laughter. Finally, the man with the strident voice spoke.

"Okay, Ames, let's have it. What'd you want to see me about?'

"Well, ah . . . the Mountain View Nursing Home."

"Construction's right on schedule. Is that what's worrying you?

"Well, no, that's not it. I've been watching it go up, and as far as I can see, it looks all right . . ."

"So what's your problem?'

"Well, ah . . . I've been told it's not up to code."

"Who fed you that rot?"

"Dale told me that . . ."

"Dale! What in the Samhill does he know about the construction business? He's nothing but a glorified book-keeper. I take my orders straight from old man Wyatt himself."

"But he said . . ."

"Now, see here, Ames, you may be the esteemed mayor of this town, but sometimes you poke into affairs that are none of your business. Better make sure you don't . . ."

Abruptly, the sound cut off. I could still hear the tape running and looked up at Sam questioningly. He shook his head.

"I played it all the way to the end," he said, "but couldn't pick up anything else." He pressed the rewind. "Would you like for me to run it again?"

"Yes, would you?" I leaned down and listened closely for anything I might have missed.

I shook my head. "Neither one of the voices sounded like my client."

"Julie," he said hesitantly, "I hope you're not going to take this the wrong way, but last night I began to wonder what you'd got yourself mixed up in and made a couple of calls." He quirked his lips, a wry smile on his face. "I got chewed out good for waking up an important official in Walla Walla, but after he simmered down, he gave me the information I asked for.

"According to him, about three years ago, Ralph Ames, the mayor of Walla Walla at that time, was shot to death in his home. The man suspected of killing Ames was never brought to trial for murder. Some kind of plea bargain was made and he spent a year or so in the Walla Walla pen for graft."

"Was his name Lahrman?"

Sam threw me a piercing glance. "Yeah, right. How did you know?"

"He's the one that left the tape with me."

"Where does Jules fit into all this? That's why you've been acting so wired, isn't it?"

Sam didn't miss much. I'd tried to appear calm the previous night, but twice I caught myself jiggling my foot up and down while I was sitting on a stool in his workshop. This morning, I found myself doing it again.

"I'm not sure," I said, answering his first question. "The only thing I know for certain is that on the morning of the day Dad died, he opened a file on Dale Lahrman, an old school mate of his.

"But I didn't find that out until last night. Late yesterday afternoon Lahrman showed up at the office, demanding to see Dad. He seemed shocked when I told him Dad had died three years ago.

"After he left, I went down to the file room and did

some checking. I found a file on Dale Lahrman, but there was almost nothing in it."

"Lahrman didn't offer a hint about why he was so anxious to see Jules?"

I shook my head. "No, he clammed up when he heard Dad was dead, but he did ask me to keep a package for him."

"Do I ask what was in it?"

"Now, how would I know that?" I grinned at him and he grinned back. Darn Sam, he knew me too well.

He walked me to the door, flipped over the window sign to read OPEN and stepped back. "Let me know if I can be of any help," he said as I walked out. A really great guy, Sam. No lectures, no advice, and if he was worried I'd do something rash, he had the grace not to show it.

By the time I arrived back at the office, it was after 8:00 A.M. Two cars were parked across the street from my door. I studied them carefully. Both of them were sedans, but neither one was the same make or model as Lahrman's.

I checked my answering machine to see if he had called. He hadn't. I locked up again and walked next door to Brio's.

Nancy was behind the counter, filling an order, but she looked up and smiled when she saw me. She slipped two loaves of bread into a paper bag and set it on the counter while a stout middle-aged woman dug into her handbag for her coin purse. As Nancy waited for payment, she motioned for me to sit down at one of the tables.

While the woman was slowly counting out her money two other customers lined up behind her. Nancy pushed a button beside the cash register. Instantly one of Sadie's daughter-in-laws stepped out of the kitchen and came to help her.

I sat down to wait.

When the brief flurry was over, Nancy brought a plate of sweet rolls over to my table and pulled out a chair. "Susan offered to take over the counter so I could take a short break," she said, sliding the plate toward me. "Have one; they're still warm." She picked up a soft fragrant bun, brown with cinnamon and heavily glazed with sugar, and bit into it. "It's the first time this morning I've had a chance to sit down."

I studied her as we emptied the plate. She didn't have a care line in her face. She kept chattering on about how busy they'd been all morning until I couldn't stand it any longer.

"Have you heard from Donny?" I asked.

"Oh, he's home with Mom. Shane brought him back last night and thanked me for letting him have some time alone with his son. He said he missed Donny a lot while he was gone." Her face colored a bit. "He said he missed, me, too."

"What about the girl he's with?"

"Oh, she doesn't mean anything to him. She's just the sister of a friend of his. He said she's a nice kid, but that's all."

"Nance, you didn't buy that, did you?"

"What do you mean by that? I just told you Shane said there's nothing going on between them."

I didn't say a word. I simply stared at her with my mouth open.

"Well, you don't have to look at me like that," she said, defiantly. "If I want to have dinner with Shane while he's home, I will. It's a free country, you know." She picked up the empty plate and marched off. I felt like running after her and shaking her, but I didn't. I merely shook my head, pushed back my chair and marched out.

A patrol car was parked on the blacktop below my porch railing. When I stepped into the foyer, a police officer was standing outside the door of my office.

"Do you work here?" he asked.

"I'm J A Ferguson," I said. "What can I do for you, officer?" He held up his badge, gave me time to inspect it and then handed me a slip of paper.

"Is that your signature?"

"Yes," I said, glancing down at a receipt from my office. Examining it more closely, I saw it was the one I'd made out to Dale Lahrman the day before. I felt a flutter in my chest, almost certain I wasn't going to like what came next.

"How well did you know this man?"

"I didn't know him at all. He stopped by my office yesterday and left a parcel in my care. He was supposed to pick it up today. Why? What has he done?"

"Ma'am, I'm afraid he may be dead. The night manager of a local motel called and told us he'd found the body of a man in one of his rooms. The deceased didn't have any identification on him, but we found your receipt in the pocket of his raincoat.

"Ma'am, we'd appreciate it if you'd go to the morgue and identify him."

"What happened? Did he have a heart attack?"

"We don't know yet, but we suspect someone may have killed him."

Chapter Five

Being a good citizen has its downside. I wanted to cooperate with the local police, but visiting the morgue with Officer Jacoby was my version of heavy duty. I tried to think of a plausible reason for avoiding it.

"I didn't really know Dale Lahrman," I said. "I'd never met him until yesterday."

"But you got a good look at him, didn't you? You'd recognize him if you saw him again?"

"Well . . . yes."

"We'd appreciate your help," he said, unsmiling. He was a tall muscular man with a commanding air about him. It seemed useless to argue; besides, I'd run out of excuses. Politely refusing his offer of a ride, I agreed to meet him at the front entrance of the local funeral home.

Though growing rapidly, our area still wasn't large

44

enough to support an independent morgue like those in Seattle or Spokane. In Richland all human remains, after being pronounced dead by the Benton-Franklin county coroner, were immediately transferred to Einan's Funeral Home on the bypass highway. I headed in that direction.

I drove through the open gates and turned right on the paved road that led to the funeral home. Off to my left I caught sight of a mound of fresh floral bouquets and wreaths, a colorful tribute to a recently deceased loved one. I couldn't help wondering how many times grieving donors had sent flowers to their departed loved ones while they were still alive to enjoy them.

Officer Jacoby was waiting for me on the walkway outside the building. Silently, we climbed the shallow concrete steps to the doorway. Inside, a soft-voiced man in a gray business suit and striped tie stepped out of a nearby room to meet us. After a cordial exchange of words, he led us down two flights of stairs with wine-colored carpeting to the lower level of the building. The overhead lighting was subdued, giving a cool shadowy feeling to the area below.

We turned into a short hallway. On ahead, the door of the holding area was open. Under the glare of white lights, I could see a row of flat, sheet-covered gurneys, all of them unoccupied. We didn't go that far.

The mortuary attendant stopped in the hallway beside a single gurney placed along the inside wall. The sheet on this one did not lay flat and smooth like the others.

"Here we are," he said. "Miss Ferguson, if you'd like to move a little closer, please . . ."

Despite my efforts to stay calm, my pulse quickened. I knew what the next few minutes would entail and I dreaded them.

I hesitated, then stepped up beside him. After all, that was my sole purpose for being there.

He drew back the sheet, uncovering the head and a portion of the upper torso of the victim. He was a man in his early fifties, broad shoulders, gray hair. His face was lacerated with unhealed cuts; one eye was puffed up and discolored; his jaw was bruised and out of line.

Involuntarily, I shuddered and my eyes squeezed shut. Officer Jacoby placed a steadying hand on my shoulder.

"Are you all right?"

I nodded, took another quick look and turned away.

"It's Lahrman," I said huskily. Although I hadn't really known the man, seeing him there, badly bruised and beaten, caused me more emotional stress that I'd been prepared for. The painful sight had renewed afresh the memory of the day when my father was the one lying on a gurney in that hallway.

"You're certain?" Officer Jacoby peered intently at my face as though searching for any sign of doubt I might have.

"Yes, I'm sure even though he . . ." I shuddered again. "Was he beaten to death?"

"So it seems. We'll know more after the autopsy." As

we talked, we moved away from the gurney. The attendant replaced the sheet and accompanied us up the stairs.

I was glad to get out of there and back outside. Yesterday's rain had cleaned the air. It smelled heavenly.

"If you don't mind, we'd like you to come in and make a statement," Officer Jacoby said. "Also, we want to examine the parcel Lahrman left with you. If you like, I can follow you home and pick it up."

"That won't be necessary," I said. "I'll bring it in with me. I'll stop by my office just long enough to take care of some personal business, then I'll come on down to the station." By the set of his face, I had a feeling he thought my personal business was something that could be postponed indefinitely, but he refrained from saying so.

As soon as he left, I went back to my office and began calling all of the telephone numbers listed under Richland motels. I was halfway through when I came to Columbia Crest Hotel. When I asked the desk clerk to connect me to Dale Lahrman's room, she gasped and hung up.

I climbed back into my jeep and drove up Swift Boulevard, then slowed down in front of the Columbia Crest Hotel and looked for Lahrman's car. I wondered if the police were aware of its existence. Officer Jacoby hadn't mentioned it.

The building was a long two-story frame building built in the early 1930's, originally a boarding house for men. About thirty years ago an enterprising businessman had covered it with lap-board siding, painted it a pale gray, trimmed it in black and hung a block-lettered sign above the doorway. A few years ago the management had undergone a change. Since then, both the building and clientele had deteriorated.

I drove slowly past it, circled the block and pulled up in front of the building. I sat with my hands on the steering wheel, letting the engine idle. In addition to my jeep and two dusty cars, the only thing in sight was a large dumpster, which was smashed in on one side and sitting at a tilt. Apparently, it had been that way a long time because the rust had crusted over the spot where the beige paint had been scraped off.

All around the building, a crop of fresh weeds had sprung up in the untended flowerless border. I wondered why Dale Lahrman had checked into such a dismal place when he came back home. Perhaps he hadn't wanted to be seen by anyone who had once known him.

I shifted into low gear and drove around the end of the building to the unlined blacktop behind. I scanned the few cars pulled up under the windows. No sign of a gray sedan. I parked, then entered the building through the door at the end. Straight ahead of me was a long hallway that led to the lobby.

By now, the police would have cordoned off the area around the crime scene, making it off limits to the uninvited, especially a lowly PI. Still, it wouldn't hurt to take a quick look around.

I managed to walk past the doors of the first floor

without anyone seeing me. I peered around me. Nothing suggested the police had been there. At the back of the building was the stairway to the second floor. I started to climb up them.

When I reached the first landing, I found the fire door propped wide open and yellow police tape across it. Immediately on my right, a police officer sat on a chair with his back against the wall. He lifted his right hand and waved me back.

"Miss, you can't come in this way. You'll have to go around to the front end of the building to come in."

"I was looking for Officer Jacoby."

"You might try police headquarters."

He was looking at me curiously as though memorizing my face. I hastily turned away, mumbling a hasty, "Thank you," as I retreated down the staircase.

Now what? A bit of nosing around the unrestricted part of the building? Why not? I stepped from the stair landing, wondering if I dared approach the desk clerk.

A few doors up the hallway a woman with a vacuum cleaner and a bucket of cleaning supplies was clomping along in my direction. She had wispy gray hair, a pale aquiline face and was dressed in faded blue cotton pants and a man's striped shirt. As she plodded toward me an alcoholic stench preceded her.

"Pardon me," I said, pasting a smile on my lips. "I wonder if you could help me. My uncle asked me to meet him here, but I can't remember his room number. I thought you might know what it is."

She looked me up and down, her face expressionless except for a sudden alertness in her eyes.

"What's your *uncle* look like?"

The way she stressed uncle, I knew she'd heard that ploy before. Surely, I didn't look like a hooker. Or, did I? Maybe these days they wore understated pants suits to come calling.

"He's about five-feet-ten with gray hair and was probably wearing his black raincoat."

She ran her tongue over her top dentures, pushed them back into place and picked up her bucket.

"Yeah, I seen him yesterday; he was checking in. I didn't pay no attention to what room he took."

"Was he alone?"

A speculative gleam came into her eyes; she glanced down at my shoulder bag, shifted the bucket to her other hand and rubbed the back of her neck.

I pulled out my wallet, took out a ten-dollar bill and held it out between my first two fingers.

Her gaze slid over my hand and dropped down to the stained green carpet on the floor. She gave it a thorough inspection, cocking her head to one side, as though wondering if it needed her attention.

I replaced the ten with a twenty and saw her eyes flick toward it. By the way she rubbed her thumb against her fingers I could see she was tempted, but not satisfied.

Ah, the price of inflation these days! I dug into my bag again and added a five to the twenty, but that was as far as I intended to go. I had my standards, too.

She held out her hand and waited until I'd placed both bills on her palm.

"He was alone. But I heard a man asking about him just before I went off my shift."

"What did the man look like?"

"Tall with whitish hair. Had on wire-rimmed glasses like one of them old timey preachers on TV."

"Did you notice anything else about him? His clothes, maybe."

"Hmm . . ." She stared down at the floor, lifted a callused hand and scratched the back of her neck. "He had on a raincoat, black, mebbe dark gray, and he was carrying one of them little cases . . ." She thought a moment. "Not a regular type suitcase, but one of them salesman kind."

"Attache case?"

"Yeah, I guess that's what they're called." She looked back over her shoulder as though fearful someone had crept up behind her. "I can't remember anything else and I've got work to do." Grabbing the handle of her vacuum, she began to push it up the hallway. She stopped at the door of one of the rooms, unlocked it and went in.

I walked on by and headed toward the lobby. A dewy-eyed redhead was sitting behind the front desk, smoothing a heavy coat of dark fuchsia lipstick over her full bottom lip. She rubbed both lips together and was peering at herself in a pocket mirror when she caught sight of me.

"Can I help you?" she asked, frowning.

"I'm looking for my uncle," I said "I was supposed to meet him here."

"What's his name?" she asked, pulling an open ledger toward her. "Is he registered here?"

"Well, I don't think he is, yet, but he was here last night to see if you had a room available. Maybe you remember him. A tall blond man, wearing a dark raincoat?"

"I went off duty at six last night. Was he in before that?"

"No, later in the evening."

"I wouldn't have seen him then. Reggie took over the desk when I left." As she began to eye me suspiciously, I decided it was time for me to leave. I edged toward the front door.

"Wait!" She stood up, her little girl voice rising in volume. "I'm suppose to check the ID of everyone who comes in or goes out of this building."

I dug into my bag, pulled out my driver's license and handed it her.

She squinted at it nearsightedly. "I'm supposed to be extra careful," she said, studying my picture and glancing up at me.

"Oh? Why is that? Have you had a recent burglary?"

She leaned across the desk, "No, worsen that," she whispered. "A man got bumped off here last night."

"Really! How awful. Do the police know who did it?"

"No, that's the scary part."

"Wow! No wonder you're being so careful about

ID's. Look, if my uncle comes in, will you call me? I whipped out the notepad I keep in my handbag, jotted down my private number, tore it off and handed it to her. "I'd really appreciate it." I lowered my voice and said in a conspiratorial undertone, "I don't think my uncle should stay here until the police catch the murderer."

She leaned her head closer and whispered, "What'd you say your uncle looks like?" I repeated the description the cleaning lady gave me of the man who had inquired at the desk for Lahrman. She licked the tip of her pencil and laboriously wrote it down, then looked up at me. "And what did you say his name was?"

The telephone beside her rang. She picked up the receiver and motioned me to wait while she thumbed through the reservation book.

Taking advantage of the opportunity to slip away, I ran out to my jeep, worried I'd already spent too much time inside the hotel. If Officer Jacoby found out I'd been here, he might come looking for me.

Chapter Six

When I walked into the foyer of my building, Gordy was pacing up and down. He didn't smile when he saw me. That was a bad sign. Normally, Gordy's a smiley kind of person.

"What's wrong, my friend?"

"It's all my fault, Julie. If I'd been here, it never would have happened. I shouldn't have listened to him, but he said they were fresh and I thought I could pick them up and get back here before you came home, only they were busy and when Nancy finally got around to me, she wanted me to sample something and . . ."

"Whoa, Gordy," I said, catching hold of his arm. "Slow down a bit. Why don't we go into my office and you can sit down and tell me what's bothering you."

"But you don't understand."

He was right about that; I didn't. He stopped pacing and pointed his finger toward the rear of the foyer.

"It's open . . . and it's all my fault."

"The door to the basement? But, Gordy, it's locked. I checked it last night before I went to bed."

"No . . . I mean, yes it was locked, but it's not now." He gulped in some air and said in a dismal voice, "Neither is your safe."

I frowned. What was the matter with him? He wasn't making any sense. I shot another glance across the foyer.

"Gordy, the basement door is closed."

"It is now," he said. "I shut it when I came back. I mean, I shut it after I saw it standing open and noticed the lights were on in the basement. That's when I went down and found your safe open."

For a moment I gaped at him, then I dashed past him, flung open the door and charged down the stairway. At a distance the safe looked undisturbed. On closer approach, I could see the door was slightly ajar. I pulled it all the way open and looked inside. The contents appeared to be in the same order as I had last seen them, except for one thing: Lahrman's parcel was no longer on the top shelf.

I pawed through the safe, pulled out stacks of legal paper and files and dumped them on the floor. I reached back in and took out my grandmother's black enameled jewelry box. Lifting the lid, I peered inside. Everything looked the way I'd last seen it, but to make certain, I hastily sorted through it. The only things of real value—the cameo, the string of pearls and the jade necklace—were still in their pouches. With a sigh of relief I tucked them back inside with the rest of the jewelry and snapped the lid shut.

Even as I went through the motions of checking out the shelves, the left side of my brain told me to stop wasting my time. Whoever had broken into the basement and skillfully managed to unlock my safe must have found what he came for. Dale Lahrman's parcel was the only thing missing. *What made it so valuable to the thief to risk a daylight raid on my basement?*

Gordy was hovering anxiously over my shoulder. "What did he take, Julie? Anything valuable?"

"He must have thought so," I said, shoving the files and stacks of papers back into the safe. "I wish I knew why."

I stood up. "Let's go upstairs and call the police. While we are waiting for them to come, you can tell me why you feel responsible for what happened down here."

Chapter Seven

"All right, Gordy." I said, replacing the telephone receiver, "the police are on the way. While we're waiting, why don't you tell me what happened when I was away from the office." As I leaned back, making myself comfortable, my swivel chair sent out a protesting squawk.

Usually when that happened, Gordy would spring to his feet and offer to give the offending spot a few squirts of silicone spray. This time he didn't even seem to notice. He was slumped down on the old leather couch by the inside wall. His shoulders were drooping as he stared down at the toes of his scuffed brown boots. He heaved a long sigh, his face the picture of a small boy who had done something naughty and was about to confess.

"I was waiting for you," he said in a forlorn voice. "You told me you might have a job for me, remember?" I nodded and he went on. "You'd left the outside door open, so I figured you wouldn't be gone long. Well, while I was waiting a man came in. He asked me if anyone was in the office and I told him you weren't, but you'd probably be back soon. So he sat down on the bench beside me and we got to talking." Gordy let out another long sigh.

"Did he say why he wanted to see me?"

"Not at first, but after awhile he asked me if any of the neighbors had a key to your office. He said you were holding a package for him and maybe if someone would let him in, he could sign for it and be on his way." Gordy glanced up at me, then shifted his eyes back to his boots. "He seemed real friendly, but he kept glancing at the door and looking at his watch. I thought maybe he was in hurry to go someplace, so I asked if you could mail the package to him, but he said he'd rather pick it up personally.

"Then I guess I asked him if it was too valuable to be mailed and he said, 'To me it is.'

"And then I guess that's when he asked me again if I didn't know someone who had a key to your office. I told him it probably wouldn't do him any good because you kept all your valuable things locked up in your safe.

"Julie, I didn't tell him about the safe being in the basement, honest."

"Don't worry about it, Gordy. So then, what happened next?"

"Well, he stopped talking about his package. He said the bakery next door looked like a nice place and wondered if I'd ever bought anything there. I said, sure, all the time. I told him they had the best baked stuff in town. He got up from the bench and said he was going over there to take a look at what they had for sale. After awhile he came back and opened the front door. He didn't come all the way in, just held the door part way open and waved one of Brio's sacks at me. I could smell it from where I was sitting. It sure smelled good. He said he'd bought some apple-cinnamon rolls. He said they were having a special on them today and if I wanted some, I'd better go over there right away before they were all sold out. So I did. Go get some, I mean. And you know the rest." His voice trailed off and he slumped back down on the couch, looking gloomier than ever.

"Gordy, tell me about the man. What did he look like?"

"He was tall and thin with medium-length whitish hair and . . ."

I swung forward, squawking my chair in excitement. "Tell me about his face. Can you describe it?"

"I didn't get a real good look at his face. He kept the lower part of it covered with his hand while he was talking."

"Was he wearing glasses?"

"Yeah. Dark-tinted granny glasses."

"Was he carrying an attache case?"

"Yeah, how'd you know about that?"

I didn't answer at once. There was no doubt in my mind the man was the same one who'd been at the hotel, inquiring about Lahrman. But who was he? I became aware Gordy was talking to me.

"Sorry," I said, lifting my head attentively. "What did you say?"

"I said if you want to see what he looks like, I can show you his picture."

"You can! How did you get his picture?"

"When he left here, I stood by the window and watched him walk up the street, swinging his bag of cinnamon rolls in his hand. When he came to the corner, he took off his glasses and tucked them into his breast pocket. About then, he turned his head and glanced back at the building. That's when I took a shot of him with my telephoto lens."

Chapter Eight

The police did a thorough job of checking out the safe, the staircase, and the rest of the basement, but the only fingerprints they found were mine. Apparently the thief, whoever he was, had worn gloves.

"You'd better have a locksmith change the combination on your safe," Detective Ross Kinney told me. "No offense, Miss, but this one is so simple a child could have figured it out. Also it'd be a good idea to have a deadbolt put on your basement door."

Detective Kinney was a big, dark-eyed man. Except for his voice, he reminded me of Tom Selleck. The detective's voice was low and throaty with a slight gravely texture, which seemed just right for him.

He picked up my grandmother's black enameled

jewelry box and handed it to me. "Will you check over the contents and see if anything is missing?"

I lifted out the red flannelette pouches one at a time and examined each piece of jewelry. After I replaced the last piece in its pouch, I shook my head. "No, I'm sure every piece of Grandma Ferguson's jewelry is still here." While I was stowing the pouches back inside, a few small golden charms dropped from a chain bracelet and fell to the floor. Ross Kinney knelt down beside me and helped me pick them up.

When my presence was no longer required downstairs, I carried Grandma's jewelry box up to the office, intending to repair the charm bracelet as soon as I had time. I would never wear it, I seldom wore jewelry, but somehow the thought of restoring it to perfect condition seemed an appropriate behavior for a loving granddaughter. Besides, maybe someday I'd have a daughter who, despite my negative influence, would take after my mother's love of such things.

My early memories of my mother, Andrea, were of a beautiful fluttery type of woman whose ears, neck and wrists were always dripping with shiny chains, pearls and crystals. I suppose in her own way my mother loved me. She gave me a quick hug now and then and bought me frilly little dresses, but she never allowed me to sit on her lap and wrinkle her pretty clothes.

My mother loved parties. I remember how happy she was when she was getting all dressed up to go out to someplace special. She always looked so pretty and smelled so wonderful. I remember how her eyes flashed with excitement when she spun around in a new dress to show it off to Dad. Dad always told her she would be the 'belle of the ball'.

But I also remember how they fought over money when they didn't know I was listening.

While I was down in the basement the office telephone had rung two or three times, but I let the answering machine pick it up. Now that I was back in the office, it seemed a good time to play them back. The first one was from Gordy, saying he'd almost finished developing the picture he'd taken of the intruder and did I want him to bring one of the copies to my office before he took them to the police station. Poor Gordy. He was trying so hard to make up for what he'd decided was all his fault.

I'd tried to tell him that if the man hadn't managed to break in this morning, he might have returned during the night while I was in bed asleep.

"Gordy, nothing was going to stop him," I said. "If he'd found me here alone, I might never have lived to talk about it." That seemed to mollify him some, especially when I added, "If that picture you took of him turns out well, the police are going to be mighty grateful to you."

The other message on my machine brought a sudden chill to my spine.

"This is Cinda Lahrman, leaving a message for Jules Ferguson. Mr. Ferguson, I haven't heard from my father since he left home yesterday. He has heart trouble and I'm worried about him. If you know where he is or if he stops by your office, please tell him I'm leaving home right now and expect to be in Richland in about an hour. Thank you."

I called information for the telephone number of the Lahrman residence in Walla Walla and immediately dialed it. The telephone on the other end rang and rang, but no one picked it up. Apparently Lahrman's daughter was already on her way. I leaned back in my chair, wishing she'd mentioned the time of her call so I'd have a better idea of just when to expect her.

I heard footsteps out in the foyer and looked up. Detective Kinney was standing in the doorway, his hand braced against the doorframe.

"We're leaving now," he said. "When can we expect to see you down at the station?"

"Come on in," I said, my finger hovering over the replay button on my answering machine. "I think you'd better hear this."

He lifted his eyebrows questioningly and stepped inside. As I restarted the message, he listened intently. When the recording ended, he was silent for a few moments.

"So Lahrman had a daughter," he said with a slight shake of his head "That poor girl. She's in for a shock."

"Do you have any objection if I wait until she shows up before I check in at the station?"

"None at all . . . just as long as you bring her in with

you. She might be able to tie up some loose ends for us." He ducked his head politely at me and strode out the doorway.

I leaned my elbows on the top of my desk and cupped up my hands to hold my chin, wondering what Dale's daughter was like. I breathed out a sigh, dreading I'd have to be the one to give her the bad news.

"Is something wrong, Julie?"

I glanced up. A hesitant Nancy was standing in the doorway.

"Nothing at the moment," I said. "Come on in." I'm waiting for someone from Walla Walla to show up, but she probably won't be here for half an hour or so. "What's on your mind?"

"I saw the cop cars outside. And then a policeman came into the bakery and asked us some questions. What happened? Are you all right?"

"I'm fine. Someone broke into my basement and opened my safe while I was gone. The police were here checking things out."

"Was anything stolen?" She slid into the chair by my desk, her eyes shiny with curiosity.

"Nothing of mine, but a client's package is missing."

Nancy shivered. "I heard a criminal always returns to the scene of his crime. Do you think that's true?"

"Not this time. I don't think you need to worry about someone prowling around this building. For some reason, he was interested in only that one package. He didn't touch anything else."

"That's really pretty," Nancy said, noticing the jewelry box on my desk. "Is it new?"

"No, it belonged to my dad's mother. Would you like to take a look at the family heirlooms?" I opened the box and shoved it closer to her chair. One by one, I lifted out the pouches. She thought the pearls were 'gorgeous,' the cameo, 'cute,' wasn't too impressed with the jade necklace, which was my favorite, but raved enthusiastically over the charm bracelet. I placed the bracelet on top of its red pouch and set it down in front of her so she could examine it more closely.

"Oh, Julie, how can you not want to wear this? If it were mine, I'd wear it all the time. Just take a look at this precious little bear . . . and this tiny teapot. Why, the lid actually opens. And see the wheels on the baby carriage? Look at them. You can spin spin them around.

"Oh, what's this sticking out of the pouch? It must have fallen off. Why it's hands, little praying hands. Aren't they darling?"

"Let me see that, will you?" She passed the tiny golden hands over to me and I inspected them carefully. "I can't remember Grandma having a charm like this on her bracelet . . . yet the hands look familiar." I handed it back to her.

"Nancy, I almost forgot . . . Gordy left a message on my answering machine. Will you excuse me for a minute while I call him back?"

Still enchanted by the large variety of intricate charms on Grandma's bracelet, she paid little attention to me as I dialed Gordy's number and asked him to stop by my office on his way to the police station. I was anxious to take a look at the man who had hood-winked Gordy into leaving the building long enough to rob my safe.

"And, Gordy, would you mind stopping by Sam's for a tape he's holding for me? I'd run over and pick it up myself, but I'm waiting for someone from out of town and can't leave." He seemed pleased I'd asked.

"Thanks, I really appreciate it," I said. "I'll call Sam and let him know you're coming."

By the time I'd finished my calls Nancy had replaced the charm bracelet in the pouch and returned it to the jewelry box. She was perched on the front of her chair, biting at the edge of her thumbnail and staring down at the floor. She sensed me looking at her and glanced up.

"Julie, I'm sorry I got mad at you the last time you came to the shop. Having Shane in town has me all upset."

"I know," I said, patting her on the arm. "How are things going?"

"All right, I guess. He always brings Donny home on time.

"Julie . . . I didn't have dinner with Shane after all."
"Oh?"

"He stood me up. I was waiting for him and he called and said he couldn't make it."

I didn't know what to say. In my book, Shane was a louse, but it didn't seem the right moment to express my personal opinion of him. Besides, she already knew what I thought.

"Maybe he had to confer with his grandfather's attorney," I said, not believing it for a minute, but she looked so wounded I felt I needed to say something to comfort her.

Before she could make a reply, Gordy barged in through the doorway, out of breath and looking a bit cocky. I was glad to see his self-image had improved. Gordy in the midst of self-abasement is a pitiful sight.

As he laid Sam's copy of Lahrman's audio-tape and a manila envelope on my desk, Nancy stood up to leave.

"You don't have to go," I told her. "Gordy is in a hurry and can't stay long. He's on his way to the police station."

"That's right Nancy," Gordy said, puffing up his chest and firming his spine. "The police are waiting for me."

"I really should go," Nancy said, moving toward the doorway. "It's nearly time for me to relieve Sadie so she can go home. Thanks for talking to me, Julie."

"Anytime," I said, wishing I could have been more help to her. Her shoulders were sagging and her face had the appearance of someone ready to cry.

Gordy left shortly after that. As soon as he'd passed through the doorway, I pulled the bottom desk drawer out a few inches, planted my feet on it and leaned back in my chair with the manila envelope in my hand. Afraid of being disappointed in Gordy's long shot, I was almost reluctant to open it.

Unclipping the flap, I slipped out two eight by ten photographs, one a full body shot, the other an enlargement of the man's face. He was tall and lean, but muscular, with whitish hair and good facial features, nose not too big, chin firm and well-angled. He might even have been considered handsome if it hadn't been for his eyes, starey protrudent eyes with pale gray irises of such a light shade they appeared almost white.

I was certain I'd never seen the man before, but something about him tugged at my memory. Or did his protruding eyes merely remind me of someone with the same problem? Unmistakably, they were the result of an over-active thyroid.

I glanced at the digital clock on my desk, wondering if I had time enough to go downstairs and search through Dad's old files before Lahrman's daughter arrived. Maybe that's where I had seen a reference to the man with the odd-colored eyes.

Before I could come to a decision, I heard the outer door open and quietly close. Soft footsteps made their way across the foyer.

Chapter Nine

My door was standing open, a habit I'd acquired while waiting for expected visitors. From my desk, I had a clear view of the foyer, which afforded me an opportunity to size up any new client who came in. I'd learned the way a person walked revealed a lot about her character. Short, halting steps suggested shyness or fear, a strong rolling gait indicated confidence, or perhaps arrogance. Even the tilt of her head gave a clue to her state of mind.

The young woman now approaching my inner doorway trod lightly, barely touching her heels to the floor. She glanced quickly from side to side as if she were checking to be certain no one lurked in the shadows. When she saw the door of my office was open, she moved swiftly up to the desk and spoke to me in a soft breathless voice.

"I'm Cinda Lahrman. I called Mr. Ferguson an hour ago to say I was on my way. Did he get my message?"

"Cinda, I'm Julie Ferguson," I said, standing up and leaning across the desk to shake hands with her. "Won't you sit down. We need to talk."

"It's Dad, isn't it?" she said with a strangled sob. "Something's happened to him."

"Please, sit down, Cinda." I gestured to the club chair beside my desk. "I think you'll find that comfortable."

She sank down into it, her legs folding as though they were no longer capable of holding her upright.

"I just knew it," she said, gently biting her lower lip to quell the trembling. "I've felt all morning something was wrong."

Cinda Lahrman was a small brunet in her early twenties with large hazel eyes and short straight hair. Despite her delicate build and present distress, I sensed she was a woman who did not easily dissolve into tears.

"Is he in the hospital?" she asked. "No, I can see by your face that it's more than that. He's dead, isn't he?"

I nodded. "Yes, I'm sorry to tell you, he is."

Lahrman's daughter crossed her arms and leaned over, clutching her chest. She rocked back and forth in her chair as though in great pain. My first impulse was to step around the desk and attempt to comfort her, but her body language told me to leave her alone. Sometimes pain needs to find its own release. I know; that's the way it happened with me.

Presently, she grew still and looked over at me, her fingers digging into the soft flesh above her elbows.

"Tell me," she said.

"It happened last night. The night clerk went to his room to deliver a message and found the door ajar. He peeked in and found him lying on the floor."

"They killed him, didn't they?"

"They? Who do you mean by 'they'?"

"Those crooks at Wyatt Construction. They testified against him and got him sent to prison, but he was innocent."

She must have thought she saw a flicker of doubt on my face, because she stiffened and spoke more loudly.

"Please, you must believe me! I knew my dad; he was completely honest; he couldn't have done what they said. Those men framed him."

She kept her gaze pinned on me, her eyes willing me to accept the truth of her statement. Whether he was innocent or not, I didn't know, but this girl apparently idolized her father, just as I had mine. I wanted very much to hear her story.

"Your father and mine were friends a long time ago," I said. "Did you know that?"

"Yes. I met your father the day he came to Walla Walla at Dad's request. He seemed nice, but he never came back, never even called to let Dad know he wasn't going to help him." She lifted her chin, gazing at me almost hostility.

"Dad was killed on his way back to Richland that

night," I said. "He didn't have a chance to help your father."

She leaned forward in her chair, her eyes wide. "Did they . . . Are they the ones who killed him?"

"I don't know.

"How did he die?"

"The police thought he went to sleep at the wheel and drove off the road. He hit a gully and flipped over. The car caught on fire."

"And my father. How . . ."

"Someone beat him up. That may have caused his death, or it's possible he might have died from a heart attack. We'll know more after the autopsy."

"I want to see him."

"I'll see what I can do." I picked up the telephone and called Detective Kinney to relay the request. After a brief interchange, I hung up and turned back to her.

"Detective Kinney said he'd arrange it. He wants you to stop by the police station. He'd like you to personally identify your father's possessions."

"Cinda, they found your father's car. It was abandoned in East Pasco. I'm afraid it's been stripped, even the tires and the driver's seat."

"It doesn't matter," she said, her bottom lip quivering a bit. "Nothing matters except Dad."

"I know how you must feel. I went through it, too." I fiddled with some papers on my desk, giving her time to regain her composure. After a short interval, I glanced over at her. She was sitting quietly in her chair, her hands lying limply in her lap.

"Cinda, there's something we need to talk about. Your father left a package with me. It contained a gun. Do you know anything about it?"

"It was mine. It was used to kill the mayor of Walla Walla . . . but I didn't do it! Neither did Dad."

"The mayor was killed about three years ago, wasn't he? What can you tell me about it?"

"It was all so ugly," she said, clenching her fists. "I'll never forget it. Never!" She sighed and dropped her hands back into her lap. "Miss Ferguson, would you . . ."

"Please call me, Julie," I said.

She nodded, a smile briefly crossing her lips. "Thanks . . . Julie. What I wanted to ask you was, would you take me on as a client?"

"What is it you'd want me to do?"

"Find out who killed my dad and see if you can put him away."

"Cinda, the police are looking into it."

"That's here in Richland. I want you to see if you can find the connection between his death and what happened in Walla Walla. Those men framed Dad and managed to cover it up. Everybody thinks they're fine upstanding businessmen, but they're not. They're a bunch of crooks." She frowned. "Unless . . ."

"Yes?"

"Maybe, it would be too dangerous for you."

I bristled; she'd hit a sore spot in my vanity. "Let me be the judge of that."

"Then you'll do it?"

"I'd need a retainer."

She didn't even hesitate. She opened her handbag and whipped out her checkbook. "How much?"

"Anything. A dollar? Later on, you can pay me whatever you think it's worth."

She dashed off a check and handed it to me. Automatically, I glanced down at it. She'd made it out for a thousand dollars. I arched my eyebrows at her.

"I don't take charity," she said.

"All right, I get your point." I passed her one of my standard forms. "Now, if you'll just sign this at the bottom—read it first, if you like—and then we're in business."

She gave the printing a brief scrutiny, wrote her name on the line at the bottom, added the date and handed it back to me. I slipped the signed sheet into my top desk drawer and picked up the pictures Gordy had dropped off.

"Cinda, please take a look at this man and tell me if you've ever seen him before." I laid the pictures down on the desk before her.

She studied them one at a time, returned to the enlarged close-up of the man's face, picked it up and examined it at length. She laid it back on the desk with the other one and looked over at me.

"No, I don't know him. Who is he?"

"He's the man I suspect of having robbed my safe of

the package containing your gun. Also, I have reason to believe he's involved in the death of your father."

She glanced back down at the pictures. "I wish . . ." She picked up the top picture and studied it again. She shook her head.

"No, I can't help you. I'm positive I've never seen him before."

I dug into the drawer where I keep my loose change and took out two quarters. I laid them over the eyes in the enlarged close-up. "He wore dark-tinted glasses," I said.

She stared down a the man's face, taking time to inspect it thoroughly, then shook her head.

I scooped up the coins and slid the pictures back into the envelope.

"I want to hear about the gun," I said, "but first, there's an audio tape I want you to hear." I snapped it into the player on my desk and turned it on.

As the first words came across, she scooted forward in her chair and listened intently. When her father's name was mentioned she glanced over at me, her eyes startled, but didn't say anything until the tape ended.

"Where did you get that?" she asked.

"It's a copy of the one that was in your father's package. You've never heard it before?"

"No, I didn't even know Dad had it."

"You recognized the voices?"

"Yes, of course. One was Mayor Ames." Her eyes narrowed and her voice took on a bitter tone. "The other one belongs to that crook, Allen Drukker."

Chapter Ten

Cinda cast a covert glance at her wristwatch, the second time in the last few minutes. I knew what was going on in her mind: she was anxious to visit the morgue and have a look at her father. So far, she had only my word he had died. Until she personally viewed his body, it would be natural for her to cling to the hope I'd made a dreadful mistake.

"Shall we go?" I pushed back my chair. "Detective Kinney is waiting at the police station to take you to the funeral home."

She shook her head. "Thank you, but that's not necessary. I've already taken enough of your time. If you'll just give me directions . . ."

"It's no trouble," I said, pulling my tote bag out of the bottom drawer of the desk. "I'd really like to do it."

And I meant it. Although Cinda appeared to be the self-sufficient type, her visit to the morgue was apt to be upsetting for her. She might need someone to talk with afterward.

I locked my office door, thinking wryly as I did so, if someone wanted to get in, he wouldn't have much difficulty with my old-fashioned locks. I made a mental note to schedule an appointment with a locksmith when I came back home.

We walked out to my jeep, bypassing the shiny red subcompact Cinda had parked in front of my building. The color and make of her car caught me by surprise. From the understated way she was dressed, I'd have pegged her for a sedate sedan in a bland shade of beige or gray.

We talked in intermittent snatches on the way through town, mostly just light remarks about the area we were passing through. We carefully avoided any mention of the ordeal ahead of her, but I couldn't help noticing how she kept clenching and unclenching her fists.

When I pulled up in front of the police station, Cinda unbuckled her seat belt before I'd even had a chance to shut off the motor. She inhaled sharply and stepped out on the pavement.

We walked inside together. I stopped at the front desk and gave the attendant our names. "Detective Kinney is expecting us."

"Please be seated and I'll notify him."

Detective Kinney appeared almost immediately. "Thank you both for coming in."

"Miss Lahrman, if you'll come with me I will take you to the funeral home and bring you back."

Before I could say a word, he turned to me. "Ms. Ferguson, I have arranged for someone to take your statement. If you'll take a seat, she'll be right out. Would you like to wait here until we come back, or shall I notify you at your office when we are through?"

Somewhat miffed about the way I was being shut out, I told him he could reach me at my office. I had just time to say, "I'll see you later, Cinda" before he whisked her away.

After the policewoman took my statement about the break-in at my office, I walked outside and climbed into my jeep.

The sun was out and a light breeze was blowing. A perfect spring day. And a perfect day to be alive. That thought stirred memories of the last day Dad and I spent together. At the time, I was still living in Seattle with my ex.

I'd tried so hard to sound upbeat every time I called Dad on the neighborhood payphone. At the time I was still foolish enough to think I had convinced him my hasty marriage was turning out beautifully. I kept rambling on about the mild weather and the great seafood restaurants and fabulous art galleries. I should have known better. He'd never had a bit of trouble seeing through any of my past subterfuges.

He appeared at my door late one morning. I stared at him blankly for a moment, the last person in the world

I expected to see when I'd heard our cumbersome lift rattling upward.

"Dad, are you checking up on me? Is that why you're here?" I couldn't help bristling. He hadn't wanted me to marry Roger and I hated for him to learn how poorly the whole sorry business was working out.

I still don't know how he found me; the only address I'd given him was a post office box number. Up until then, I'd always skillfully dodged his questions about our 'apartment' by claiming it was only temporary. I'd never been able to muster enough courage to admit we were living in a condemned wharf-side loft only a few blocks from Pike Street Market. The seaminess of our living quarters never seemed to bother Roger. Not even the smell. With a window open, the wind from the sea rushed in, carrying with it the overpowering stench of dead or decaying fish.

"No, no, Julie, don't misunderstand," Dad said. "I had to come to Seattle on business. Fortunately, I was able to take care of it last night, which gave me this opportunity to look you up while I was here. I would have called first if you'd had a telephone." In one swift glance, he took in my scrubby surroundings, which had defied my every effort to make look habitable.

"I'm glad I caught you in," he said, the expression on his face revealing nothing of what he must have been thinking. "If you're not booked up for lunch, I'd like to take you out somewhere and swap news.

"Roger, too, if he'd like to go." As he was talking, I

saw his keen eyes taking in the metal sculptures standing about on the uncarpeted floor, none of which were finished and some with merely a piece or two joined together.

"He's out," I said, shortly, "attending to some personal business and I'm not sure when he will be back."

"Well then, put on your face, honey, and let's the two of us go out on the town, that is, unless you're ashamed to be seen in the company of your old man."

"Dad! Stop talking like that!"

We had a wonderful time. We drove out to the University district and ate lunch in some little drop-in-place in the Village Square. Afterwards, we browsed in the small shops nearby and I let him buy me a huge green fern to hang from one of the rafters in the loft.

That evening we shot up the side of the Space Needle in its bullet-shaped cage and ate a leisurely dinner in the restaurant, watching the changing lights and scenery as we slowly revolved. I can't remember all we talked about; I remember mostly that we laughed a lot. As he left me at my door, he enveloped me in a tight hug.

"If it gets too rough, honey, come on home."

I wished I had.

I started up the jeep, intending to go back home, but thinking of Dad had made me restless. I drove up George Washington Way to Swift Boulevard and on impulse drove straight across the by-pass highway into the cemetery. I parked in the middle lane and walked across the newly mown grass and stopped by a flat granite gravestone. I knelt down, brushed off a few blades of grass and then stood up, gazing silently at Dad's name.

I've known people who spent hours on their knees by a grave, carrying on a one-sided conversation with a departed mother, husband or brother. They all claimed to have come away refreshed. It never worked that way for me. I always felt closer to Dad while sitting behind his desk with one foot planted firmly on the bottom drawer, just the way I'd so often seen him do.

I hurried back to the jeep and climbed in and headed home.

About an hour later, I heard a car draw up in front of my building. I walked out into the foyer and looked out.

A police car stood in front of the porch steps. The passenger door was open. Detective Kinney was solicitously helping Cinda out. He walked up the steps with her and opened the outside door.

By then I was back in my office, sitting at my desk. I looked up as they walked in.

Cinda's eyes were red-rimmed and slightly puffy, but she seemed completely composed.

"Do you have a place she could lie down for awhile?" Detective Kinney asked. "We'll need to see her later this afternoon."

"Of course . . ."

Cinda interrupted me. "That's not necessary," she said. "I don't want to bother Julie. I can easily check into a motel and be available when you need me."

The detective peered at me over Cinda's head. "I

want to talk with both of you. It would be better if you came in together, but that's up to you." He turned and walked out.

We stared at his retreating back. The good detective had had the last word.

"Have you had lunch?" I asked. I'd missed mine and was starting to feel weak in the knees.

"No, but I'm not sure I could eat anything right now."

"Let's go upstairs, shall we? It's quiet, and you could sit down and relax while I brew a pot of coffee and fix us something to eat. Tuna salad okay?"

Tuna salad was a specialty of mine, one of the few things I could serve without worrying about how it would turn out.

"Yes . . . but, please, I don't want to cause you a lot of work."

"You won't be," I said. "I can toss it together in no time."

I showed her where the upstairs sitting room and bathroom were, then excused myself to go back down and check my answering machine. I thought Gordy might have called to crow about his interview with the police. There was only one message on the machine, but it wasn't from Gordy. The voice was low, raspy and obviously disguised.

"Tell Cindy Lou to keep her trap shut if she knows what's good for her.

"And the same goes for you, Julie Ferguson."

Chapter Eleven

When I went back upstairs, Cinda was lying on the sitting room couch with her knees drawn up and her eyes closed. As I started to slip away, she raised her head and stared at me, blinked her eyes a couple of times and sat up.

"I'm sorry," she said. "I must have dozed off."

"Rest as long as you like. We're not on a definite time schedule."

"No, I'm ready to get up."

"In that case, coffee's ready and the salad is made. I hope you don't mind informal dining," I said, ushering her down the hallway, "because the kitchen table is the only one I have."

"The best kind," she said, a faint smile relaxing the somber line of her mouth.

I'd made up my mind not to tell her about the threatening message on my answering machine until after we'd eaten lunch. She seemed to be coping well with the sudden death of her father, but with these quiet types, you never really knew what was going on in their minds.

She sampled the tuna salad, then took a second bite. Despite her earlier claim not to be hungry, she began to eat as though she were starved. She also devoured two of the hot rolls, which were fresh out of Brio's oven and still warm and moist. I wondered if she was really that hungry or if she were one of those people who stuffed themselves when they were overwrought.

After we had finished our salads, I cleared away our empty plates and refilled our coffee cups. At the same time, I set down a small platter of bar cookies.

"I couldn't eat another . . ." Cinda's voice trailed off as she took a closer look at the cookies. "Those look wonderful," she said. "Did you make them?"

"I wish I could claim them, but I have to confess they're from Brio's Bakery next door. If you like raspberries, try the one with the red filling. The butterscotch ones are good, too."

For a short while we talked like two old friends who had met for a coffee break, then reality set in again and our gay mood vanished. After a few minutes, I broke the silence.

"Cinda, we need to talk. Do you feel like telling me about the gun?"

She nodded, took another swallow of coffee and set her cup down. She sat quietly, staring down at the cookie crumbs on her place mat, apparently marshalling her thoughts.

"My boyfriend gave me the gun," she said, softly. "I was attending Whitman College at the time and was in the habit of walking home after classes. I didn't live on campus. It wasn't necessary because my home, my parent's home actually, was only a few blocks away.

"In the winter it gets dark early and there are shadows around the buildings and under the trees. I was crossing the campus late one afternoon when all of sudden I had the feeling someone was following me. Every time I stopped and looked back no one was in sight, but when I started up again, I could hear movement behind me. It wasn't the first time this had happened, but up until that afternoon I hadn't given it much thought. There's lots of activity on campus, students hurrying back and forth between the buildings or sauntering out to their cars. I just naturally thought it was someone going in the same direction as I was.

"But that day was different. It was abnormally cold out, the temperature near freezing, so no one was dawdling along like they sometimes did.

"I began to walk faster. The grass on the ground was crisp from the cold and the footsteps behind me were clearly audible. I glanced around once and saw someone duck behind a tree. I panicked and broke into a run. I don't know when he stopped chasing me, but at some point along the way, I became aware no one was following me anymore.

"When I reached the safety of my doorway, I began to rationalize. Maybe I'd just been imagining things. I'd lived in that neighborhood all my life. I just couldn't believe anything sinister could happen in such peaceful surroundings."

She picked up her coffee cup and sipped quietly, draining it before she set it down on the table and gazed sightlessly into it. I sat unmoving in my chair, reluctant to offer her a refill for fear I might break her train of thought.

"Two days later," she said, "I was going home from choir practice, when the same thing happened again. I mentioned it to my boyfriend, Ken, and that's when he gave me the gun to carry in my purse.

I didn't want to take it; I've always been afraid of guns. But Ken insisted. He took me out into the country and taught me how to use it and showed me how to take it apart and put bullets in it. I still didn't like the idea of carrying it around in my purse, but he said most of the time it wouldn't be necessary. Then he put his arms around me and said, 'Honey, please take it along with you when you have to walk home in the dark. I worry about you.'

"My parents were out of town at the time. When they came back I showed the gun to Dad. I'd never seen him so upset.

" 'Cinda, I don't want you walking home by yourself,

not even in the daytime. If you can't find a ride home with someone you know, call me or your mother and one of us will pick you up.'

" 'But, Dad . . .'

" 'No ifs, ands or buts,' he said. 'If someone is stalking you, we can't be too careful. Now, get your coat on, we're going down to the police station and report this.'

"When Dad was worried about me, he tended to treat me like a child. I didn't really mind. It was just his way." Her eyes misted and she reached into her handbag for a tissue.

I stepped over to the coffeemaker and picked up the glass serving pot. I didn't want any more coffee and maybe Cinda didn't either, but I refilled both of our cups, giving her time to pull herself together. It didn't take long; Lahrman's daughter seemed to have a lot of resilience.

"I suppose you want to know how my gun became the one used on Mayor Ames."

"I'd like to, yes."

"Someone stole my purse," she said almost defiantly. She peered over at me, her eyes demanding to know whether or not I believed her.

I met her gaze evenly. "How did that happen?"

"I really don't know. I was attending a lecture and had placed my bag under my seat like I always did. After the lecture, I reached down for it and it was gone."

"The gun?"

"No, my whole bag. By the time I discovered it was

missing, everyone in the row behind me was already filing out. I couldn't see it in anyone's hand and nobody around me was acting in a suspicious manner. I checked the seats all around me, thinking someone might have accidentally kicked it away with his foot.

"Finally, I went on to my next class. Afterward, I walked slowly up Boyer Street, waiting for Ken. His last class was the same time as mine, so he always caught up with me and walked me home.

"I heard someone call out my name. Thinking it was Ken, I looked around, but I didn't see him or anyone else. I became frightened and began running along the sidewalk. I could hear footsteps pounding along behind me. They seemed to be gaining on me, so when I came abreast of Mayor Ames's house, I dashed across his lawn and rang the doorbell.

"He was home and let me in. Did I tell you Mayor Ames was a good friend of my father? They were golfing partners and served on some of the same charity boards. They always got along real well together . . ."

She stopped and peered out the window, a glazed look on her face. After a few seconds she shook her head as if to clear it, and sat up straighter in her chair. "Now, what was I talking about?"

"You were at the mayor's house. You'd just lost your purse."

"Yes . . ." She drew in a deep breath and continued on. "I sat talking to the mayor for awhile and then called Dad at his office. He said he had some work to finish, but that it wouldn't take long and then he'd drive by and pick me up. As it happened, Joseph, the mayor's son—he was still in high school at the time—drove up in his souped-up car and offered to take me home. He let me out at the end of my driveway and roared away.

"As I walked toward the front steps, I noticed a dark object lying in the shrubbery. It was my handbag. My first thought was that someone had found it in the lecture room, discovered my identification inside and dropped it off at my house. But that seemed odd. Why hadn't he taken it up to the door? I quickly opened it and checked inside. The small sum of money I carried around with me was still there. So was my credit card.

"But not the gun. I dug frantically through my handbag again. There was a small rip in the lining that I'd been intending to fix, so I thought the gun might have slipped down through it. I patted my hand across the bottom and was checking along each side when the front door opened. My mother looked out at me.

" 'Cinda? Why are you standing out there in the cold? I heard a car pull away some time ago. Who brought you home?'

" 'Joseph Ames gave me a lift.' I stepped inside, still rummaging around in my handbag. 'I couldn't find my house-key.' I didn't tell her about the gun. I decided to wait and talk it over with Dad when he came home.

"But by that time, the mayor was dead and Dad was in trouble." She glanced down at her wristwatch and then over at me. "Shouldn't we be going to the police station?"

"You're right, we should. We can talk on the way, but first, there's something I think you should hear." She threw a quizzical look at me.

"It's a message that came in on my answering machine. It concerns both of us."

I hated to play the tape back for her. She'd already had more than enough emotional stress for one day, but I had no right to keep it from her any longer.

Cinda sat on the edge of her chair with her head bent down over the answering machine, listening to every word. She held up well, no shivers, no cries of fear. The only trace of emotion I noticed was a slight narrowing of her eyes when her name was mentioned.

"I wonder who it is," she said when the brief message had played out. "The voice is so distorted."

"Did the speech pattern or any of the words he spoke suggest anything to you?"

"Only my name. Allen Drukker always called me Cindy Lou. It irritated me and he knew it."

"That's not your name?"

"The name on my birth certificate is Lucinda Louise, but I've never been called anything but Cinda by my family and friends."

"How did he find out what your full name was?"

"I don't know except . . ."

"Yes?"

"Well, Drukker has a way of finding out things. It's

rumored he has his own personal spies in all the key places around town." While we were talking I took out the answering machine tape and dropped it into my tote bag.

On our way to the police station, I stopped by Sam's and asked him if he had time to make a speedy copy of my tape.

He nodded and retreated to his workshop. A few minutes later he came out and handed me two tapes: the original from my answering machine, and the copy he had just made.

"Thanks, Sam. I owe you." As I opened the door to leave, a thought struck me and I stepped back inside.

"If you made a copy for yourself, please clue me in if you come up with anything."

A fleeting grin passed across Sam's face. As our eyes met, he favored me with a downward nod of his head.

Chapter Twelve

After tucking the tapes into the side pocket of my tote bag, I drove up Swift Boulevard until it connected with George Washington Way, made a right turn and continued up the street to the police station.

I turned into the parking area and pulled up in front of a low brick building with a concrete barrier running across the front. To the left of the entrance, white letters spelled out the words: City of Richland. Below them, foot-high letters captioned the one word: POLICE.

I unbuckled my shoulder strap and pulled the keys out of the ignition. As I dropped them into my tote bag, I glanced over at Cinda. She hadn't moved. She was staring through the window at the building, a quiver in her lower lip.

"Cinda, we're here," I said, quietly.

She nodded, drew in a deep breath and released her shoulder strap. Side by side, we walked into the building. A row of chairs sat under the windows in the waiting room. I motioned to them.

"Why don't you sit down and rest while I notify the front desk we're here?"

I'd barely had time to walk back across the waiting area before Detective Kinney and Officer Jacoby stepped out of a door on our left and walked over to us.

"Thank you both for coming in," Detective Kinney said. "We'll try not to keep you here any longer than necessary.

"Miss Ferguson, I'd like to take your statement first, so will you come with me, please?

"Miss Lahrman, Officer Jacoby has some articles for you to look over while you are waiting."

Detective Kinney unlocked the solid door at the left of the waiting area, stepped back to let me pass through and then led me down the hallway to his office.

As I sat down across the desk from him, I reached into the side pocket of my tote bag and handed him the two tapes. The first was the original from my answering machine, the one that contained the threat from the unknown caller; the second was a copy of the tape that had been in Lahrman's package. When I described the contents of that one, Kinny gave me a sharp, searching look and wanted to know how I had come into possession of it.

"I had a backup copy made," I said, hoping my tone

of voice conveyed the impression that to do so was just part of my normal office procedure.

"In case of emergencies?" he asked, giving me a knowing grin.

"Something like that," I said, smiling back at him.

He let it go at that, probably because without it, he'd have had no clue as to why someone believed Lahrman's package was important enough to steal. Kinney still hadn't heard about the gun. That was a story he needed to hear from Cinda.

He turned on his recorder and went over my story carefully, extracting every detail I could remember from the time Lahrman unexpectedly showed up at my office through the events that had occurred after Cinda arrived at my door. When he was through questioning me, he asked me to wait out in the entryway while my statement was being typed up for my signature.

As he escorted me to the door, I saw Linda in the hallway with Officer Jacoby. She tried to smile at me, but her lips scarcely lifted before they closed down again. Poor girl. It has been a long, tough day for her and it wasn't over yet.

A few minutes later, I spotted Officer Jacoby talking to the officer at the front desk. I went over to the window and asked him when Lahrman's autopsy was scheduled. At first, he didn't answer me, and I thought maybe he didn't intend to.

"It's going on now," he said and strode away before I could ask him anything else. Somehow, I had the feeling

Officer Jacoby wasn't too happy with me. Maybe it wasn't personal. Maybe he just didn't like female PIs.

Nearly an hour passed before Detective Kinney summoned me back into his office. I slid a glance at Cinda. She was sitting in the chair beside his desk, intense fatigue written in the slump of her shoulders and the set of her face.

"I've asked Miss Lahrman not to leave town for the present," Kinney said. "I understand you offered to put her up at your place."

"Yes, I did."

"I think that's a good idea. That way, we can keep an eye on both of you at the same time."

"I don't need . . ." His eyebrows lifted; an amused look appeared in his eyes. I didn't finish my sentence. True, I didn't need any police protection; I could take care of myself, but Cinda . . . Well, that was another matter. I might not be able to watch over her every minute, not when I'd already planned to do some sleuthing on my own.

"That'll be fine," I said lamely. He smiled at me, a long languid smile that made goose bumps slither up and down my spine.

On the way back to my house, Cinda seemed tense and withdrawn. A faint frown marred the smoothness of her forehead and occasionally her lips moved soundlessly.

When I spoke to her, she seemed not to hear me, then raised her head and glanced over at me.

"I'm sorry. Did you say something?"

"Yes, but it wasn't important. We have only a few more blocks to go, then you can lie down and rest." We traveled the rest of the way in silence.

I turned my bedroom over to Cinda and moved a few of my personal necessaries into Dad's old room. I'd contemplated giving that room to her because it was larger than mine, but I feared the oversized furniture and the deer head on the wall might be intimidating to someone like Cinda. Besides, it gave me an excuse to sleep in Gram's old four-poster bed. Not that I couldn't have anytime I wanted to, of course, but I'd always entertained the notion that to do so would diminish Dad's presence in the room.

After I'd stashed my personal things away, I went down the hall to the kitchen and rummaged around in the freezer and pantry for the ingredients needed for our evening meal. Whenever I was in a cooking mood, I made up big batches of spaghetti sauce loaded with herbs from my walled in garden behind my house. I stored the sauce in the freezer along with a few loaves of garlic bread and my special homemade apple cake. Boil up a pot of pasta, toss a salad and I was ready for guests. So far, no one had ever complained.

When I looked in on Cinda, she was sitting on the bed, holding something in the palm of her hand. She turned it over with her fingers and examined the other side. Under the glare of the ceiling light, I could see it was a small golden trinket.

"Oh, I thought I'd put all those away," I said, stepping

into the room. "It was my grandmother's; it dropped off of her charm bracelet."

"No, not this." Cinda looked up at me, a puzzled expression on her face. "I just now took it from under the lining of my handbag. I sewed up a big rip in it ages ago, but a small section of it has split open again. This must have lain hidden under the lining for at least two years. I wonder . . ." She frowned. "But that doesn't make any sense."

"What doesn't?"

"That it might have been in there ever since my gun was stolen." A shiver passed over her. "Julie, something strange happened at the police station. While I was identifying my father's things, Officer Jacoby held up a little plastic bag with something in it that looked like this. I told him I'd never seen it before." She glanced down again at the golden trinket in her hand. "It must be just a coincidence."

"May I see that, please?" I held out my hand, a chilling feeling rising in my body.

She passed the trinket to me and I studied it closely. It was a pair of praying hands, exactly like the one Detective Kinney had found on the floor by my safe. Handing it back to her, I barely managed to keep my fingers from trembling. Maybe my mind was creating ripples in a smooth stream . . . but I doubted it. Two times could be a coincidence, but three? No way.

"Excuse me." I backed away from her. "I'd better check on dinner."

"May I help?" She stood up to accompany me.

"No," I said hastily as I moved away. "Thanks, but everything's under control. I just want to stir something on the stove and then run downstairs for a minute. After that, we can eat."

I gave the spaghetti sauce a hasty stir, reduced the heat to warm and dashed downstairs to the basement file room. Dropping down on my knees before the bottom drawer of one of the steel file cabinets, I pawed through the manila envelopes. The one I wanted was three-fourths of the way back. I pulled it out, carried it over to the table and dumped out the contents: a varied assortment of sympathy cards and letters that were sent to me after Dad's funeral service.

From among them I selected an ordinary white envelope, the only one addressed to me in thick block letters with no return address in the upper left-hand corner. I turned it upside down and shook it over the table. A shiny golden object tumbled out. It was small, almost flat, and shaped like hands folded in prayer.

Chapter Thirteen

I drew a strand of spaghetti out of the boiling water and tested it between my teeth. Perfect. Quickly draining the pasta, I heaped it on two warm plates and ladled on the meat sauce. As I was sprinkling freshly grated parmesan cheese across the top, Cinda entered the kitchen. She'd freshened up for dinner. Her soft brown hair was now smoothed back from her forehead and tied at the nape of her neck with a pale blue scarf, emphasizing her triangular, almost childish chin. She'd washed her face and removed her pale mauve eye shadow and ice-pink lipstick, making her appear pathetically young and very, very tired.

Cinda claimed the spaghetti smelled wonderful and tasted delicious, but as she went through the motions of eating, she seemed to withdraw into herself. I had the feeling she wasn't even aware of what she was eating or that I was sitting across the table from her. Now and then she drew in a deep breath as though she had just remembered to breathe.

I sat quietly, slowly winding my spaghetti around my fork, my mind still in shock at what I'd discovered in the file room. The tiny pair of praying hands Cinda had found in the bottom of her handbag and the one Detective Kinney had picked up by my safe were identical to the pair mixed in with the sympathy cards for my father.

What did it all mean? Was it a conspiracy of some kind?

I clearly remembered the day that particular envelope arrived in the mail along with some other cards and personal messages from clients and friends. At the time I hadn't attached any special significance to the little golden trinket inside. It was just someone's unique way of expressing sympathy, I'd thought, someone who had forgotten to enclose a name. It had never occurred to me the omission might have been deliberate. As the full significance of the act hit me, my hand dropped limply to the table, my fork clattering against my plate.

Cinda glanced up, a startled expression on her face.

Raising my napkin to my mouth, I coughed a couple of times as though I had choked on my food. She didn't look convinced.

"Julie, are you all right?"

I nodded, coughed once more into my napkin and laid it down. I picked up my glass of burgundy and took a sip. "What's your personal opinion of this?" I asked, hoping to divert her attention. "It won a gold medal last year, also best of show."

"Julie, what's wrong? Ever since you turned your bedroom over to me, you've been acting strangely. I'm afraid my staying here is too much to ask of you. I really think it would be best if I went to a motel."

"No, please don't do that. You're not the problem; it's something else. I plan to tell you about it, but before I do, I'd like to hear what happened two years ago in Walla Walla. You mentioned your father had been framed."

"Yes, it was awful." Tears welled in her eyes. "Poor Dad, he suffered so much and now . . ."

She dabbed at her tears with her napkin, making a concerted effort to steady herself. "I told you about my handbag being stolen, remember?" I nodded. "Well, it was all part of a scheme to set Dad up. Of course, I didn't find that out until much later on. By then, it was impossible to prove I wasn't lying about the gun being taken from my handbag by some unknown person. Everyone, even the judge, seemed to think I was just making up a story to protect Dad." She leaned back in her chair, no longer making any pretense of eating.

"What really happened that night was this: after Joseph Ames and I left in his car, someone broke into his house through a rear door and shot his father. A short time later, Dad drove up, found the front door standing wide open and walked in. When he saw the mayor lying on the floor, Dad knelt down beside him. While he was feeling for a pulse, someone slipped up in back of him and hit him on the head, knocking him out. When he came to, my gun was in his hand. Still groggy from the blow, he stumbled out the door and drove home. He looked ghastly when he staggered into the house."

She shuddered, a far away look on her face, as though the scene was still fresh in her mind. "He was pale and shaky and there . . . there was a splotch of blood on his coat sleeve.

"My mother ran over to him and asked him what was wrong. He brushed on past her, saying he had to make a telephone call. We heard him punch in three numbers and ask for the police. He told them he was coming down to the station to report a crime. Then he left the house. I ran after him; I wanted to go with him, but he wouldn't let me.

" 'No!' he said. 'I want you to stay home with your mother. Ralph is dead and I don't want you getting mixed up in this mess.'

"I was stunned. I thought he meant the mayor had committed suicide. Later on, I leaned the truth of what had happened."

"What about the gun? Did he leave it at the scene?"

"I'm coming to that!" It was obvious, my interruption had unsettled her because she pressed her napkin tightly against her lips and dropped her head down over her plate, breathing deeply.

I sat there quietly, studying the side of her face and

observing the unnatural paleness of her skin. Poor girl. She'd endured a long, stressful day, and probably had more questions thrown at her than she was emotionally prepared to handle. I was sorry I'd ever opened my mouth.

I slid back my chair and started to gather up the plates. She placed a restraining hand on my arm, her eyes pleading for my understanding. I laid the plates back down on the table and sat down again.

"Dad didn't have the gun with him when he came into the house," she said, her voice sounding weary but steady. "I asked him about it later and he told me he'd hidden it close by, along with an audio tape Mayor Ames had given him earlier that day."

I didn't say anything, but she must have read the question in my eyes because she said, "No, he never told me where he'd hidden either the gun or the tape. I guess we'll never know unless . . .

"Julie, when he left that package here with you, did he say anything that might indicate . . ." She broke off when she saw me shake my head.

"No, the only thing I can tell you is the package had soot on it. Does your house have a fireplace?"

"Yes, but I don't think he could have hidden it there when he came home. I would have noticed. My mother and I were sitting in front of the fire when he burst inside, and after he called the police station he immediately left the house.

"Oh, I wonder . . ." She paused, frowning. "Our next

door neighbors have an outdoor fireplace they haven't used in years. They're an elderly couple and seldom go out into their backyard. I suppose he could have stored the gun and tape in their chimney." She gave a slight shrug of her shoulders. "I guess it doesn't matter now where he put them." She stared at the table, absently brushing a few breadcrumbs together with her fingers.

"After Dad went to the police station and told them about Mayor Ames being murdered, they sent a team out to the Ames' house to verify the mayor's death and search for evidence. That was when they discovered the lock on the rear door had been forced open, but whoever it was didn't leave any fingerprints there or anywhere else in the house.

"They questioned all of the neighbors and one of them, Richard Raebum, testified he had heard two gunshots about five thirty that evening, and then seen Dad's car pull up in front just a few moments later. That seemed to clear Dad of any wrongdoing.

"But that didn't stop Drukker and his cohorts. They managed to frame Dad for graft." She reached for her water glass, took a few swallows and then set it down again.

"I want to tell you the rest of it, and then if you don't mind, I'd like to go to bed."

"Yes, of course. You must be exhausted."

She managed a weak smile and then took up her story again.

"Wyatt Construction Company is owned by my grandfather, John Wyatt, and the main headquarters are located in Spokane. At the time all of this happened, Dad was manager of the Walla Walla branch and Allen Drukker was just a crew foreman. Dad became suspicious that Drukker was taking kickbacks from some of the suppliers for allowing them to substitute inferior materials for the ones ordered. Some of those materials were being used in a new nursing home. Dad planned to report proof of this to Grandpa just as soon as he and his new wife returned from Europe, but in the interim he decided to tell Mayor Ames what was going on. Dad was confident the mayor could find some way to halt construction until Grandpa came back home.

Somehow, Allen Drukker managed to turn the whole thing around. One of his men slipped into Dad's office one night and inserted false information into his computer. It made it look as though Dad was the one that was taking the kickbacks. Drukker even got one of his men to testify against Dad in court.

"Julie, Dad went through so much heartache. I really do hope you can find some way to prove his innocence and clear his name."

"I'll surely try," I said. I meant it, too. I just hoped the girl's faith in her father was justified.

The office telephone rang. It rang four times and stopped when the answering machine took over. A few seconds later my private line rang. I picked up the kitchen extension and heard Sam Bellamy's voice.

"Julie, the only thing I can tell you about the tape from your answering machine is that the voice pattern doesn't match up with either one of the voices from that first disk you brought me." I must have made an exasperated sound because a short rasp of air erupted over the line, which was as close as Sam ever came to laughing aloud.

"Not what you wanted to hear, I gather," he said.

"No, but thanks for letting me know. It eliminates one possibility."

"Sure. Anytime."

Before I replaced the telephone on the wall, I punched in Gordy's number.

"Are you ready for another surveillance job?" I asked, quickly adding, "It would be out of town. You'd have to spend a few days, maybe even a week or two in Walla Walla."

Chapter Fourteen

Cinda and I had finished breakfast and were dawdling over our last cups of coffee when Gordy's midnight blue van drew up in front of the building. I ran downstairs and let him in. Gordy was all smiles. He loved surveillance work, it gave him an acceptable excuse to snoop.

I briefed him on what I wanted him to do, then added, "But, Gordy, you don't need to go over to Walla Walla until tomorrow. Wyatt's Construction is not open on Sundays."

"No problem," he said, pacing restlessly. "I won't bill you for today. My plan is to drive around and get the feel of the town before I do any work on the case."

"Okay, then," I said, eyeing his short rotund frame, which was far from undernourished, "you can put your

108

dinner tab on the expense account. But, Gordy, lunch is on you. Right?"

"Right!" He grinned widely and scooted out of the office. I watched him speed off in his van, wondering if I had been wrong to offer him this particular assignment. At times, his enthusiasm for a project overrode his common sense and he took unnecessary risks.

When I went back upstairs, Cinda was pouring detergent into the dishwasher. The kitchen was spotless and more orderly than I usually kept it. When I complimented her, she looked surprised. "You made dinner and breakfast. It's only right that I do the cleaning up."

Cinda was fast becoming my idea of a perfect housemate.

"I need to make some long distance calls," she said, switching on the dishwasher. "Is it all right if I use the sitting room phone? I'll put them on my credit card."

"Of course. Make yourself at home. I'll be downstairs in the file room if you need me for anything."

At the doorway I paused. "You mentioned going to the funeral home this morning to finish up arrangements. Call down to me when you're ready to leave."

"Thanks, Julie, but you don't have to take me. Now that I know the way, I can go on my own."

"Do you have a cell phone with you?"

"No . . ."

"Then I think we'd better stick together. At least for the time being." Seeing the hesitant look on her face, I added, "If you're worried about me sitting in the car waiting for you, don't give it another thought. In my line of work, you get used to it. Besides, it'll give me time to do some in-depth thinking."

A smile, thin but real, momentarily lit up her face. "All right, you talked me into it. Say, an hour from now?"

"Sounds good." I left her at the sitting room door and dashed downstairs. One hour wasn't nearly as much time as I needed to plow through all of Dad's old files, but it would allow me the opportunity to examine some of those that looked the most promising.

The computer system had been added to the business only a year or so before I took over. Dad had entered all new and recent information into it and I'd continued on where he left off, but neither one of us had attempted to include any of the data from files more than three years old. There was just too much of it.

I checked the computer memory to see if there was anything listed under totems or MO's, but found nothing helpful. I closed down the computer and attacked the file cabinets, starting with the most recent records and working backwards.

My hour was nearly up when I came across something that looked interesting. While Dad was still on the police force, he'd been responsible for capturing a notorious arsonist. His name was Jofu Medina, a real unsavory fellow who enjoyed setting fires in public buildings regardless of the time of day.

After his trial, where he'd been found guilty on five counts, Medina made a death threat not only against the judge and jurors, but also anyone else involved in bringing about his incarceration.

Dad had testified against Medina in court.

Medina was now serving a long sentence in the State Penitentiary at Walla Walla. Or was he? I made a note to check it out.

When Cinda called down to me to let me know she was through with her telephone calls, I hadn't found anything else that looked worth following up on. There were still a few cabinets I hadn't touched yet, but they'd have to wait.

I switched off the lights and ran upstairs.

As we climbed into my jeep, I saw a patrol car pass by. I'd also noticed one slowly cruising past my building during the night before.

I glanced over at Cinda. Busy strapping on her seat belt, she didn't appear to be paying any attention to the street traffic. It was just as well. Arranging for her father's body to be transferred to Walla Walla would be stressful enough without being reminded of the anonymous warning that had been left on my answering machine.

All of the parking slots directly in front of the funeral home were occupied, so I double-parked near the entrance and let her out.

"I'll try not to be gone long," Cinda said, stepping out of the car.

"Don't worry about me; take all the time you need. As I mentioned earlier, I have some thinking to do."

I found an empty space at one end of the parking lot

and pulled into it. Leaning back in my seat, I pondered the injustices of life. If Dad's records were correct, Medina was still alive, still eating and sleeping at taxpayer expense while his victims, some dating back as much as fifteen years, lay moldering in the ground. Was it possible he'd had a hand in arranging Dad's accident? Probably not, but sometimes inmates found a way to reach beyond their bars.

Hmm . . . Whom did I know that might be able to reach in the other direction and supply me with some current information on Medina?

Jack Blakey? Sonny McAbee? My old friend, Marlene? Hmm.

I was still mulling over my list of possibilities when Cinda walked out of the building.

She wasn't alone. A dark-haired man had opened the door for her and was now accompanying her down the steps. Apparently he said something that pleased her because she tipped back her head and gave him a radiant smile. At the bottom of the steps, they crossed to one side of the concrete pad and stood there talking. I could now see the man was Detective Kinney.

They certainly were taking a long time about it. I wondered what they had so much to talk about. After a while they began moving again, walking slowly in my direction.

I straightened up behind the steering wheel and watched them approach. Detective Kinney seemed to be enjoying Cinda's company as much as she did.

When they came up to the passenger side of my jeep,

Kinney opened the door for her. As she slid into her seat, he dipped his head down and smiled across at me.

"Good morning, Miss Ferguson." Before I could answer, he shifted his attention back to Cinda. "All set?" he asked. After making certain her shapely nylon-covered legs were safely tucked inside, he shut the passenger door and strode briskly back the way he had come.

"What was that all about?" I asked Cinda, trying to maintain a casual tone of voice.

"Detective Kinney was concerned about my going home today. He seemed to think I'd be safer staying here in Richland. He's such a thoughtful person, so warm and considerate." She gave a quavery sigh. "And so terribly handsome, don't you think?"

"Oh?" I said, a little surprised at her exposing her thoughts about him to me.

"Yes, I guess he is?" I pulled up at the stoplight and glanced over at her. Her head was cast down, her long brown lashes lowered, hiding the expression in her eyes. A bemused smile tugged at the corners of her lips.

"What else did the two of you talk about?"

"What? Oh, nothing much." She raised her head and stared out the window, the soft dewy look no longer on her face. "He said he'd call me when the final results of the autopsy came in."

The traffic light turned green. I eased across the intersection, too annoyed at myself to look at her again. I shouldn't have grilled her about Detective Kinney; the man was just doing his job.

Chapter Fifteen

"Thanks for being so nice to me, Julie. I don't know what I would have done without you."

"I'm sure you would have managed perfectly," I said, touching Cinda lightly on the shoulder, "but I was glad to be able to help." We were out in front of my office building, standing by her car. Despite my plea of waiting until tomorrow she insisted on driving back to Walla Walla immediately after we'd finished our lunch.

"I have so much to get ready at home," she said. "Some of Dad's relatives will be driving in tomorrow, and I'm afraid I left the house in rather a mess."

I doubted that. Cinda was one of the tidiest persons I'd ever met.

Watching her drive away in her shiny red compact, I wondered about her last remarks. So much to get ready, she'd said; Dad's relatives will be arriving. It sounded as though she and her father had been the only ones living in their house. Where was her mother? Why weren't she and Cinda supporting each other during this dreadful ordeal?

Perhaps her mother was ill. If so, why hadn't Cinda mentioned it?

At the far end of the block a metallic gray sedan pulled away from the curb and fell in behind Cinda. I stepped out into the street to keep both cars in sight. The sedan followed about two car lengths behind her all the way up the street and slowed down as she approached the George Washington Way intersection. When the light changed, Cinda turned right. The sedan speeded up, made a short stop at the intersection and followed her around the corner.

I ran over to my jeep, jumped in and screeched out of the parking strip. I streaked up the street, dodging a slow-moving Ford station wagon as it was pulling away from the curb. The driver blasted irately on his horn.

I was sorry I'd scared him, but I didn't slow down. I swung onto George Washington Way and headed south, scanning the vehicles ahead. The gray four-door was two blocks ahead of me, but I couldn't spot Cinda. I wove rapidly through the traffic, swinging back and forth between the lanes. Brakes squealed; horns honked. The driver of a fiery red Camaro flipped me an obscene gesture when I whipped around his car close enough to sear the paint.

The gray sedan was only three cars ahead of me when it suddenly braked and turned onto a side street. I craned my neck as it went around the corner, but couldn't see the driver through the dark-tinted glass.

I peered up George Washington Way. A blue and white police car was cruising along in the inside lane just a pace behind Cinda's little red car. Apparently, someone in authority was looking out for Lahrman's daughter. I didn't even care to know who it was.

I dropped back and headed home, anxious to return to the basement and comb through the rest of Dad's old files.

With a notepad and pencil close at hand, I dug in, jotting down the details on anything unusual Dad had encountered while working on a case. Although the list was lengthy, I found nothing that connected him to Dale Lahrman. In fact, I couldn't find any mention of the man except for the brief file outlining his political aspirations.

I stood up and stretched. Six hours had passed and I needed a break. I began to think about dinner and a quick workout in the exercise room.

Or a test of skill.

An aluminum stepladder was leaning against the inside wall of the file room. I picked it up and set it down below an overhead grating that to a casual observer would appear to be nothing but an oversized heat register. I mounted the four bottom rungs and reached up, slid back the grate and fished around inside the opening for the unattached end of a long rappelling rope. I pulled it down, letting the free end drop to the floor. After I'd moved the ladder back against the wall, I grabbed the rope with both hands and positioned my feet. Hand over hand, my feet swinging along below me, I began to climb. Inching constantly upward, I passed through the former dumbwaiter shaft into a small open area, a section of the coat closet in my office.

Momentarily I paused, drawing breath, then continued on up to the next level. Swinging sideways, I extended one foot out, searching for the ledge. My toes found it and held tight. One at a time, I planted my feet, and then moved my right hand from the rope. Clinging to a metal hand bar at the side of the shaft, I slid back the trap door that opened into the exercise room.

I stepped out and leaned over, resting my hands on my lower thighs. It irked me to find I was panting. I hadn't realized I was so out of practice.

When my breathing returned to normal, I did a few deep knee bends, stood up and headed for the kitchen. I switched on the overhead light and opened the refrigerator, feeling an urgent need for nourishment. I dug around, found two stalks of celery and half a brick of sharp cheddar cheese. While munching on the celery, I sliced off a big slab of the cheese and slid it between two slices of bread.

While wolfing down my sandwich, I peered up at the wall clock. It was only 8:35 P.M., certainly not too late for a telephone call to Walla Walla. I lifted the receiver and dialed Information.

"MA Stelling on E Sumach, please." As the automatic voice recited the number, I jotted it down, then pushed down the button and dialed again.

The phone rang only twice before a husky voice on the other end of the line said, "Hello?"

"Marlene? This is Julie . . . Julie Ferguson in Richland. I need a favor."

Chapter Sixteen

Cinda had spent only one night in my bedroom, but in that brief time, she'd managed to leave her imprint on it. The room was now so tidy it was depressing. Not a bump or a wrinkle marred the smooth surface of the bedspread and the ruffle along the bottom of it was meticulously aligned with the pale blue carpet on the floor. The pile of books that had been lying on my night table was now neatly stored away in the bookcase. Even the frilly lampshade was hanging perfectly straight, the tear in the fabric pinned so it wouldn't show.

Now that the room was bared of its comfortable clutter, I saw it for what it was: a sentimental parody of a young girl's dream room. White French provincial furniture, flounced bedspread and chair covers, pastel prints on the walls, ruffled curtains at the windows;

each of them an end product of one of my mother's raids on the family budget, and her last attempt to rescue me from becoming a tomboy.

I plucked out the books Cinda had relegated to the bookcase and carried them down the hall to Dad's old room. Flipping on the lights I gazed about me, breathed a satisfied sigh and flopped down across the old four-poster bed. The deer head stared down at me with baleful eyes.

"Sorry, old fellow," I muttered, drowsily. "Your sojourn in this room is about to come to an end."

Much later the ringing of the telephone awakened me. Groggily, I picked up the receiver and dragged it to my ear.

"Hello?"

"I saw him, Juliet! I saw him out at Wyatt Construction Company. He . . ."

"Whoah! Hold on a minute, Gordy." I rolled over and switched on the table lamp. The digital alarm clock read: 12:35 A.M. I sat up in bed, now fully awake. Not once since Gordy had started working for me had he called me in the middle of the night. *Why now?*

"Okay, now tell me, whom did you see? The man who broke into my safe?"

"Yeah, that's what I'm trying to tell you. He and some redheaded guy came out of the plant office about nine-thirty and stood there talking under the overhead light. When he left I followed him . . ."

"You followed him? That was dangerous. Gordy, I don't think . . ."

"No, wait. I didn't mean I followed the blond guy. I couldn't have pulled in behind him without blowing my cover, but as soon as he was gone, I tailed the man he was talking with, the guy with the red hair. He was a big dude driving a GMC three-quarter ton pickup, green with black and white racing stripes. A beauty, and man, what power! He barreled out of there so fast I had a heck of a time catching up with him, but finally I managed to slip in behind him as he headed east on Rose Street. He cut over to Boyer, and then hung a right onto a short side street near the college. He stopped in front of a big white house. Just a minute; I wrote it down." A rustle of paper; Gordy mumbling to himself. "Oh, yeah, I got it now. It was 531 Marrion Street.

"531 Marrion! Are you sure? That's the Lahrman residence."

"Yeah, I know. That's why I decided to call you."

"Good thinking. Now, tell me what happened next. Did he go up to the door?"

"No, he pulled in across the street and sat there for quite a while, watching the house."

"Could you tell if there was anyone at home?"

"Oh, sure. The downstairs lights were on and three cars were parked out in front."

"Good. That means Cinda should be safe enough for the present. Anything else happen?"

"Well . . . I'm not sure; it might not be important, but I thought I'd better tell you about it. When the guy finally pulled away from the Lahrman house, I followed him on Isaacs Avenue to a bar. I went inside and spotted him sitting with a blond woman in one of the back booths. They talked awhile and then came out together. He walked her to a car, a white Cadillac with Oregon plates, then climbed back into his pickup and went home. At least I guess it was his home because he pulled into the garage and then a few minutes later, I saw a light go on inside the house. About ten minutes after that, the light went out. I waited around awhile, but when he didn't come out again I came on back here to the motel to call you. Is there anything else you want me to do?"

"Did you manage to get any pictures?"

"Naturally, that's what you sent me here for, wasn't it?"

"Yes, you're right, I did. Thanks, Gordy, I appreciate what you're doing, but be careful, won't you? Those may be dangerous men you're tailing."

"Don't worry, Julie. I can handle it." I could almost hear his chest puffing up.

"I'm sure you can. But, please be careful, anyway." I yawned. "Let's both get some sleep now and we can talk again later. I plan to leave here for Walla Walla early in the afternoon. If you're not in your room when I arrive, I'll leave a message for you with the desk clerk." After Gordy finally hung up, I rolled over and went back to sleep.

The following morning I was seated at my desk, clearing up some paper work when Lee Thompkins walked in. He told me he'd just finished filming an interview at the Federal Building and had a little time to kill before reporting back to the TV station.

"Can you take time out for an early lunch?" he asked, smiling down at me. I liked his lop-sided grin. Lee was a good guy, even-tempered, kind, lots of fun when we were both in the mood for fun, but still good company when we had other things on our minds.

I glanced down at my watch: 11:05 A.M. "Let me take a look," I said, flipping through the stack of papers on my desktop. I pulled one of them out and laid it aside, then stacked the rest of them in my standing file.

"Yes," I said, looking up at Lee, "I'd love to have lunch with you. I have only that one letter that I must send out today; the rest can wait until I get back in town."

"Leaving town? Business or pleasure?"

"A funeral in Walla Walla. An old friend of my father's.

"Anyone I might know?"

"No, I don't think so," I said as I locked the office door.

We climbed into his van and drove out George Way to a restaurant that had just been opened up. It was a cozy-looking place with subdued lighting and comfortable booths in shades of dove gray and a soft medium blue. Large potted plants were strategically placed around the room to give diners an intimate feel.

A dark-haired girl in a white shirt and trim black pants led us to a secluded corner and handed us menus. After she'd taken our orders, Lee leaned back against the soft cushion behind him and gazed over at me, a quizzical look in his eyes.

"What have you been up to since I last saw you?" he asked. "Are you still checking up on that rodeo bum?"

"No, something else is keeping me busy." I filled him in on the details of the burgling of my basement and raid on my safe. I also mentioned having a new client, but didn't tell him who it was. I knew Lee well enough to know he could keep a confidence, but since Dale Lahrman's death was now a police matter, I thought it best not to mention my involvement with it. I had no doubt Lee would hear about it, perhaps already had, but I wanted to be able to tell Detective Kinney with perfect honesty the information hadn't come from me.

Several times while we were eating, I caught him glancing at me with an unreadable expression on his face. Usually, I'd have asked him what was on his mind, but this time my female intuition told me it might be more prudent to keep quiet.

On the way back to my building, he kept the conversation light and impersonal. I thought that's where he'd leave it, and was unprepared when he jumped out on his side of the van and accompanied me up the front steps. He walked across the foyer with me and stood silently behind me while I unlocked the office door. He followed me inside and closed the door behind us. Catching me by the hand, he drew me closer.

"What's going on, Julie?"

"What do you mean?"

"I feel a distance between us. Care to tell me why?"

"Lee," I said, placing my hand gently on his arm. "I guess I haven't been very good company today. The funeral in Walla Walla is for an old friend of my father. He was killed a few days ago and I'm afraid there might be a connection to what happened to my Dad. I don't really know yet, and I'm a bit confused right now."

"Would you like to talk about it?"

"Not today, but perhaps later on. I hope you can understand."

"Sure, I do. I'll wait until you're ready to talk. Just remember, I'm here for you whenever you need me."

"Thanks, Lee, I won't forget."

He leaned over and wrapped his arms around my shoulders, then gave me a tight squeeze. It felt good.

Chapter Seventeen

When I left Richland, not a police car was in sight, nor had any been patrolling my street the night before. Apparently, once Cinda Lahrman had been escorted safely out of town, my welfare was no longer of any interest to the local police. That was the price for being an independent woman, I suppose. Everything has its flip side.

On the way to Walla Walla a light rain fell, then cleared up and the sun came out, making everything look fresh and new. I passed a hill dotted with wild yellow flowers sparkling in the sunshine. I had an urge to stop the car and take a closer look at them, but then I thought of Cinda waiting for me and drove on.

Approaching Walla Walla, I watched for the exit that would take me into the center of town. I knew if I turned off too soon, I'd find myself wandering through the industrial area, or if I waited too long, I'd bypass the downtown business section entirely and have to backtrack.

Peering up the highway, I spotted the Second Avenue exit and turned in. Second Avenue took me past an old red brick building, which early in the twentieth century was one of three bustling railway stations in Walla Walla. As railroad commerce diminished, the station was shut down. A few years ago, it was converted into a restaurant and gift shop. One of the old railway cars sat in back of the station and was often open for meals.

Farther along the street, I passed by the old Marcus Whitman Hotel, a Walla Walla landmark since 1928, now restored to some of its former grandeur.

I stopped at the red light at the corner of Second Avenue and Main Street, turned left and drove east through the center of town. When I was about nine years old Dad took me with him when he went to Walla Walla on business. I had been fascinated by the picturesque old buildings in the downtown area and the little creek running under the bridge in the center of town.

Dad told me Main Street had once been a narrow dusty trail used by pack trains and Indians on horseback. Later on, as the population increased, there had been buckboards, stagecoaches and the doctor's horse and buggy. Now, it was a wide paved street filled with modern automobiles. Despite that, some of the aura of the old pioneer days still remained.

The Travelodge Motel was situated at the end of

Main Street at the point where it intersects Isaacs Avenue. I drove slowly past the motel parking lot. When I didn't spot Gordy's van, I circled around the block and turned in at the Pioneer Inn.

The Pioneer Inn was composed of two rows of cedar-sided buildings separated by a grassy strip and a dozen or so ancient buckeye trees. I'd stayed there before. The price was right and the amenities good.

After I'd checked into a room, I called Marlene Stelling's home telephone number and left a message on her answering machine. Next, I called Cinda.

"Julie? I was wondering when you'd get into town. Have you had lunch? We've just finished, but there's plenty of food left."

"Thanks, Cinda, but I had lunch before I left home. How are you doing?"

"Fine. Dad's relatives are here. We've been busy."

"Cinda . . . are you really all right? No anonymous phone calls or anything?"

"No, nothing. I don't imagine you've found out anything, yet?"

"Nothing of importance, but I'm having dinner tonight with someone I hope can give me some information that will help. I'll call you if I learn anything new.

"Oh, by the way, I'm staying at the Pioneer Inn if you want to reach me."

"Julie . . ." A hurt tone came into her voice. "I thought you were going to stay at my house. I saved a room for you."

"Thanks, Cinda, I really appreciate the thought, but I plan to be in and out of my room a lot of the time and may be getting some late-night phone calls. For the present, this arrangement works better for me."

"But you'll be at the funeral tomorrow, won't you?"

"Of course, I will." I heard a woman's voice in the background and then apparently Cinda covered the receiver with her hand, because the sound of her voice was muffled. Within a few seconds she came back on the line again.

"I'll see you tomorrow then," she said, abruptly, signaling the end of our conversation. After we hung up, I sat there a minute, wondering about the sudden change in her manner.

I didn't dwell on it long, figuring if it concerned me, I'd find out soon enough. After I'd carried my overnight case into my room, I walked the three short blocks to the Travelodge and left a note for Gordy.

He still hadn't contacted me when it was time for me to leave for my dinner date with Marlene.

Marlene was a full ten minutes late. I was standing in the lobby of the restaurant when she burst through the doorway, looking just the way I remembered her from our college days, a tall, broad-shouldered woman with a prominent nose, a wide mobile mouth and a definite swagger to her walk. Her dark brown eyes were bright, inquisitive and exuded intelligence. Also she had one of the most forceful personalities I've ever encountered.

"There you are!" she cried, pinning me in her arms,

hugging me nearly tight enough to crack my ribs. "You haven't changed a bit, Julie. Same sexy eyes and figure you had in college. Oh, how I hate you!"

"I've missed you, too," I said, with what little breath she hadn't already squeezed out of my lungs.

She beamed down at me and gave me another rib-shattering hug. "Let's make this a celebration, shall we?" Without waiting for an answer, she propelled me toward the cocktail lounge. "My word, what a day! College students never gave me half the grief I'm getting now. I should have stayed in Honolulu."

Previous to taking the position of Director of Recreation at the state prison in Walla Walla, Marlene had been on the faculty at the University of Hawaii.

As we walked into the dim, smoky interior of the lounge, she spotted a server and called her over. "I'd like a double Tanqueray on the rocks with a twist of lemon," she said, and turning to me asked, "What'll you have, hon?"

I hesitated, not really wanting anything to drink, yet hating to refuse when it seemed to be of some importance to her.

"I'll have a spritzer," I said to the young woman patiently waiting for me to make up my mind. I was a little apprehensive about the way the evening was headed, but needn't have worried. Marlene didn't guzzle her drink as I'd feared she might. Instead she sipped it almost daintily while she plied me with questions about what I had been doing with myself since I dropped out of college to marry that 'adorable little sculptor.'

Adorable is not a word I would have used to describe my ex-husband, but I didn't tell her that. I brought her up-to-date, skipping lightly over the details of my turbulent marriage with Roger. When she started to probe a little too deeply into my personal life, I decided it was time to put her on the receiving end.

"Why did you leave Hawaii?" I asked. "I thought you loved it there."

"It became too confining," she said through taut unsmiling lips. She flipped back the right sleeve of her gray pinstriped jacket and glanced down at the plain, but elegant, gold watch on her wrist. "Let's adjourn to the dining room, shall we?" It really wasn't a question.

We were shown to a table that overlooked the garden area, now filled with clusters of red and yellow tulips. By the time we were seated, Marlene was her jovial self again. She wasn't really a pretty woman, but she had style. She wore her thick brown hair clipped short, her only adornment an expensive-looking gold pin clipped to the lapel of her designer suit. Anything else would have been an overstatement, but then, Marlene always had been endowed with fabulous clothes sense.

She and I, along with Tiffany Weathers, a charming waif of a girl with pale green eyes and soft brown curls, had been roommates at Central Washington State University during our freshman and sophomore years. After I transferred to the University of Washington in Seattle to be near Roger, I hadn't kept in touch with either one of my old friends. At the time, there was no room in my life for anyone but Roger.

Marlene and I stopped talking long enough to glance over the menu. After we had placed our orders, Marlene dipped into her briefcase and pulled out a folder containing several sheets of paper. She slid one of them across the table to me.

"That's a photocopy of a picture Josu Medina's attorney took of him about three years ago. Medina was in the infirmary at the time, following a knifing incident. You can see the slash marks on his face. He was also stabbed in the gut."

I studied the picture, committing it to memory. Medina was sitting on the side of his bed, his thick hairy legs bare. Only his stubby toes were touching the floor. He was stocky in build, short-armed and short-legged with a swarthy complexion and thick black eyebrows that stood up in scraggly tufts over the bridge of his wide flared nose. His thick lips were pulled to one side by a scar that cut down across his jaw and disappeared into the folds of his neck. He was so repulsive to look at I couldn't help shivering.

Marlene slid another photocopy across to me.

"That's a picture of the man who occupied the bed next to Medina. The two of them became real friendly while they were in there. Legally, his name is Gerald Winston Oslo, but most of the 'insiders' knew him only by his nickname—Deacon.

"He's out, now," she said, tapping the picture with her

forefinger. "But recently I've been hearing rumbles about him. I expect we'll be getting him back before long."

There was no need for me to study Oslo's picture. A single glance told me it was the same pale-eyed man Gordy had photographed outside my office. The only difference was that in this picture his eyes looked even more protruding than in the close-up shot Gordy had taken of him.

"I'm almost sure this is the man who broke into my safe," I said. "What can you tell me about him?"

"He was a collection agent working for Fidelity Finance Company in Spokane until he got a little overzealous one night and broke the arm of one of their clients. While he was 'inside,' he found religion, or so he claimed. I heard he carried a Bible around with him and quoted scripture to anyone who would listen. He spent hours in his cell, kneeling by his bed, praying."

"You mentioned hearing rumbles about him."

"Yes." She leaned across the table and lowered her voice. "What I'm about to tell you is strictly off the record and I don't know how much of it is true. According to what I heard, Oslo was let out on probation about three years ago. He worked in a warehouse for a few months, then was fired for preaching on the job. The other employees claimed they couldn't get any work done with him telling them they were all instruments of the Devil and needed to repent. Since then Oslo has had no apparent employment, but he manages to dress expensively and drives a big car. I checked with Fidelity, but they said he's not on their payroll anymore. So far, no one has been able to pin anything on him." She eyed me curiously.

"What's your interest in him? Are you trying to nail him for robbing your safe?"

"That's only part of it. I think he may be involved in a vendetta of some kind, possibly one initiated by Medina."

"No kidding! What put that idea into your pretty little head?"

We stopped talking as the waitress approached our table with our dinner salads. As soon as she was out of earshot, I answered Marlene's question, telling her first about my father's connection to Medina and then mentioning a possible tie-in with Dale Lahrman's death.

"So that's why you wanted some information on Lahrman." She took another piece of paper out of the folder and handed it to me. "This is all I could find on him." As I scanned it, she went on talking. "Apparently, he was a model prisoner, kept to himself, did what he was told and caused no trouble.

"Now, what are you frowning about?" she asked, halting her forkful of romaine a few inches from her mouth.

"I see you've listed only one visitor with the same last name, his daughter, Cinda. Are you sure he didn't have any other family visitors? He had a wife, you know."

"No, I didn't know. But if she's not listed, she never came to see him. Some of them don't." She pointed her fork at me, making short jabs at the air. "Some women can't stomach seeing their men locked behind bars, actually makes them physically ill.

"And then there's the other side of the coin; there's the poor woman who's actually tickled to death to have him tucked away and no longer able to beat up on her and the kiddies." She stuck her fork back into her salad and stabbed viciously at a slice of mushroom.

"Gad! Why are some human beings so despicable?"

The vehemence in her voice startled me. I glanced up, studying her face. It looked both angry and sad. I had a feeling that at the moment, she wasn't thinking of the inmates of the state prison, nor their women. I'd wager her remark had been prompted by something more personal. Perhaps something connected with the real reason she had left Hawaii.

The waitress slid a sizzling steak and a side of cottage fries in front of Marlene, then skirted the table and set down my plate of grilled salmon dressed in a wine-tarragon sauce.

"How you can stand all that goo is beyond me," Marlene said, slicing off a portion of her steak and lifting it to her mouth.

"Heart food," I said, forking up a portion. "I want to live until I'm ninety."

"Good grief! Why?"

"Why not?" I said and changed the subject.

Later, while we were dawdling over coffee, she told me what little else she'd been able to find out about Medina and Lahrman. None of it seemed important, but I filed it away in my memory to mull over later.

When I returned to my motel, Gordy was parked

down the street, waiting for me. He hopped out of his van and trotted toward me.

"I figured you'd want to see these pictures," he said, waving a manila envelope at me.

"I surely do." I pulled out my room key. "Let's go inside and spread them out under the light."

As usual, Gordy's pictures were excellent. The ones of Oslo showed him with his glasses on, hiding his eyes, but the rest of the details were perfect.

The shots of the red-haired man surprised me. He appeared to be in his late twenties or early thirties, much too young to be a contemporary of Dale Lahrman. I'd been so sure the other man Gordy had spotted at he construction office was Allen Drukker that I hadn't even considered anyone else.

"This man looks too young to be the manager of Wyatt Construction," I said. "I wonder who he is. You say you followed him to his house?"

"Yeah." Gordy puffed up his chest. "I tailed him all the way out Pleasant Street to a great big three-story house. Maybe he didn't live there, but it was the Drukker place all right. When I got back to the motel, I checked the telephone directory and the only Drukker in town lives at that address."

As I picked up the last picture, Gordy came around behind me and peered over my shoulder.

"Julie, I'm sure sorry I couldn't get a better shot of that woman. She kept hiding her face like she didn't want to be seen."

Chapter Eighteen

The funeral service for Dale Lahrman was scheduled for 11:00 A.M. I left my motel room shortly before 10:30 and drove out Popular Street to the mortuary. It was a handsome three-story white building with tall columns across the front portico and lead-paned windows framing the doorway. Originally, it had been the home of one of the wealthier pioneer families that had settled in the Walla Walla Valley, but like many of the old mansions in the area, it had long ago been taken over by a business enterprise.

I parked across the street to watch the mourners arrive, wondering if one of them had been instrumental in Dale's death. A cream-colored sports coupe caught my attention, mainly because the lone occupant sat hunched down in his seat with the motor running.

Reaching into the back of my jeep, I grabbed the pair of high-powered binoculars I always carried along with me. After adjusting the lens for distance, I focused on the front window of the coupe. The man inside had red short-cropped hair and chiseled features and appeared to be about twenty-five years old. That was all I could see of him except for the top few inches of his shoulders, but I needed no more than that to identify him. He was the man Gordy had followed to the Drukker residence.

A few minutes before 11:00, I locked my car and walked across the street. I was wearing a dark gray suit, gray pumps and a white silk blouse, the same clothes I'd worn to my father's funeral. Somehow, it seemed fitting.

I signed the memorial book in the vestibule, then entered a large high-ceilinged room and took a seat near the back. Off to my right, filmy peach-tinted draperies covered a row of tall majestic windows; soft hymnal music flowed out from speakers near the front.

I was dismayed at the limited number of funeral guests. Small isolated groups were swallowed up by rows of empty seats. Had most of Dale's friends deserted him when he was sent to prison? It certainly looked that way.

As the service began, I glanced behind me to see if any latecomers had arrived. The young man from the cream-colored coupe was slouched down in the last row in a seat near the doorway. He was staring intently at the curtained-off area where the Lahrman family was sitting.

Later on in the service, I heard the door behind me softly open and close. I peered around. He was gone.

At the end of the service, I fell in behind the short procession of cars that was headed for the cemetery. Following behind the black limousine, which held the Lahrman family, were three sedans and a Lincoln Town Car. I was the last in line with Gordy's van trailing nearly a block behind.

Earlier the sun had been shining, but now as we entered the cemetery and wound down the narrow paved lanes, a cloud cover moved in, blotting out the light and the warmth. A slight breeze picked up, causing one edge of the graveside canopy to flap up and down.

For the first time that morning I saw Cinda, small and neat in a navy blue dress and jacket. She was standing at the graveside, staring down at her father's flower-covered coffin. Clutching her left arm was a small shrunken woman dressed in black, an old-fashioned toque covering her hair and ears. A tall gray-haired man with a Van Dyke beard stood on the opposite side of the casket. Beside him, a dumpy little woman in a dull brown suit was dabbing at her eyes with a crumpled handkerchief. The last member of the Lahrman party was a blond woman of about thirty-five. She stood apart from the others, as though isolating herself from the proceedings. A few other women and two men stood by themselves outside the canopy.

During the short graveside service, a prickly feeling came over me. I gazed about, studying the terrain and the huge pine trees scattered throughout the graveyard and among the tombstones. Seeing nothing unusual, I faced front again, but the uneasy feeling didn't leave me.

As the Lahrman party started back toward the parked cars, the rest of us followed quietly behind them.

A woman walking near me stumbled and pitched forward; I caught her by the arm before she could fall. Momentarily distracted by her words of gratitude, I nearly missed hearing a low masculine voice call out pleadingly.

"Cinda, please . . ."

I hadn't seen from which direction the man had come. Suddenly, he was just there, walking toward her.

Cinda lifted her head, her eyes blazing and the flat palm of her hand extended toward him. "Stay away from me," she cried. "Just leave me alone."

For a few moments, the young red-haired man stood there, gazing at her with a stricken expression on his face, then he seemed to wilt under the fury of her eyes. Dropping his head, he backed away and haltingly walked off across the grass.

Chapter Nineteen

The limousine that carried Cinda and her family back to her house traversed the streets at a much faster pace than it had on the way out to the cemetery. I followed along behind it for a few blocks then took a short cut back to my motel, anxious to know if Marlene had left a message for me. I'd asked her to try to find out if there was any way by which Jofu Medina might have contacted 'Deacon' Oslo since he'd been out of prison.

No one was at the front desk when I walked in, so I rang the bell on the counter. A male clerk of thirty or so stepped out of the room behind and asked if he could be of assistance. When I asked him if there'd been any message left for me, he pulled a plain white envelope out of a pigeonhole and handed it across the counter. I ripped it open and quickly scanned the typewritten note inside. I inhaled sharply and read it again, then took a closer look at the outside of the envelope. "Ferguson" was printed on the outside, dashing any hope of mine the desk clerk had made a mistake.

He was walking away when I summoned him back. "I'm sorry to bother you," I said, my voice louder than I'd intended, "but I wonder if you could tell me when this envelope was bought in and who delivered it."

"Let me think," he said, tapping his forehead with his fingertips. "I was checking someone in . . ."

He bent over his ledger, "Yes, here it is. Someone dropped it off about eleven-thirty. I was busy and didn't pay much attention to what he looked like. Seems like he was wearing a baseball cap of some kind. Blue . . . maybe it was green. I'm sorry, I just don't remember. Why? Is it important?"

The faint clink of china and the spicy smell of chili floated out through the open door behind him. Anxiously, he glanced back into the room. He was trying hard to remain pleasant, but it was obvious he was much more interested in his unseen luncheon partner than a prolonged conversation with me.

"There was no signature on the message," I said, quickly, as he was edging away, "and I can't figure out who could have written it. Can you recall how tall he was? Color of his hair? Anything at all that might help identify him?"

"No." He paused a moment, his brow knit in thought, then shook his head. "I'm afraid I don't remember anything else about him except the baseball cap. As I said, I was busy and didn't pay much attention to him."

I thanked him and walked outside. Sagging against the doorframe, I read the note again. *Your business here is finished. Go home before someone gets hurt.* I drew in an angry breath and exhaled noisily. I hated anonymous letters and telephone calls. It was so difficult to judge whether you were dealing with a harmless wimp or a real psychopath. Also, it annoyed me that someone knew where I was staying. That meant someone had either followed me to my motel or called around until he found out where I was registered.

I climbed back into my jeep, drove around the building and parked in front of my room. Now that someone had discovered where I was, there was no longer any reason to park out of sight. I glanced about me as I climbed out of my car, but no one except two little girls on inline skates was in sight.

My presence in Walla Walla was making someone nervous. Why? What was he afraid I might uncover? Of one thing I was certain: no one was going to scare me off that easily. I wasn't leaving here until I found out what was making that unknown person nervous enough to threaten me.

I placed a long-distance call to my office telephone. None of the messages left on my answering machine sounded ominous and none of them seemed important enough to need an immediate response. Although the one from Nancy was disturbing: "Julie, please call me the minute you get home." Her voice was tremulous. Had she been crying? If so, no doubt Shane was the cause. With his fragile ego, a man like him couldn't be trusted. Nancy had wounded his pride when she divorced him and it wasn't in his nature to forgive and forget. I'd be relieved when he was back on the rodeo circuit again.

Before I left the hotel to drive out to the Lahrman residence, I took my father's .38 out of my handbag and checked it over. Not that it needed any attention, I always kept it perfect condition, but just the feel of it in my hand was reassuring. I'd used it for target practice plenty of times, but I'd never fired it at anyone and hoped I'd never have to. Still, there was no harm in being prepared.

When I turned onto Marrion Street, three cars were lined up in front of the house and two more were sitting in the driveway. I parked on the opposite side of the street and walked across.

Cinda met me at the door.

"Julie, I'm so glad to see you. Please come in and meet my family." She led me across a large comfortable living room decorated in a skillful blend of antiques and modern lounge furniture. An elderly woman in black was sitting near the hearth of a red brick fireplace. Someone had kindled a blazing fire, and yet in spite of the blazing heat, the old woman was huddled down in her wingback chair, a wool afghan draped around her shoulders.

"Great Aunt Lydia, I'd like to introduce my good friend, Julie Ferguson. Her father and mine went to high school together."

"Is that so?" Her thin puckered lips parted, exposing sparse yellow teeth. "Come closer, dear, and let me look at you. My, what a beautiful head of hair." She peered nearsightedly to one side of me, and then the other.

"Where's your husband, dear?"

Without waiting for me to reply, she swung her head sideways. "Cinda," she said in her high reedy voice, "Isn't this the girl that has all those little babies?"

"No, Aunt Lydia, that's Meredith. Julie lives in Richland. She came over for the funeral."

"Well, she ought to have a husband; every girl ought to have a husband."

A tall man walked up behind Cinda and touched her lightly on the shoulder. She turned and smiled up at him. I immediately recognized him as the tall man with the Van Dyke beard that had been at the cemetery.

"Uncle Paul, I'd like you to meet my friend, Julie."

His handshake was warm and firm and his smile appeared genuine. He exchanged a few light remarks with us then excused himself and headed toward the staircase.

"He's going up to check on Aunt Penny," Cinda said, "She's in bed with a dreadful headache."

Cinda motioned toward the adjoining dining room. "Please, come and have something to eat."

As we started across the room, she noticed an elderly

man and woman standing by the front door, gazing in her direction. She rested her hand briefly on my arm and lowered her voice. "I must go over and say good-bye to the Wilson's. You're not planning to leave right away, are you? I need to talk with you."

"No, I can stay as long as you wish."

"Oh, good. Why don't you fill your plate and I'll be right back." She hastened off to the waiting couple.

I walked on into the dining room to wait for her. On a starched white linen cloth, a beautiful buffet lunch had been spread out on a long Duncan Phyfe table. A low floral arrangement of red roses and white carnations was highlighted by an overhead crystal chandelier. As I picked up a luncheon plate from the end of the table, I saw before me enough food to feed many times over the small number of people sitting or standing about the room eating. What a shame more people hadn't shown up to honor Dale. If anyone ever needed support right now, it was Cinda.

A few steps ahead of me, a young mother was shepherding three towheaded boys around the table. She leaned down and whispered to one of them, "Tony, don't heap so much on your plate, dear."

"But, Mom . . . I'm hungry."

I sensed a motion behind me and turned around. Cinda was rushing across the floor, her gaze on the woman with the three little boys.

"Meredith, thank you for coming." The two women lifted their arms and hugged each other tightly.

"I'm so sorry about your father," Meredith said. "He was a really nice man."

"Thank you," Cinda said, a quiver in her voice, then she turned around and motioned to me. "Julie, I'd like you to meet my best friend, Meredith Anderson.

"Meredith, this is Julie Ferguson from Richland. Her dad and mine went to school together."

After a few cordial words exchanged among the three of us, I moved on down the table to give the two friends time to talk privately with each other.

I went back to the table and surveyed the salads: shrimp, potato, pasta. A gelatin and fruit mixture. A large relish tray. No tuna. As I was deciding what to take, a woman stepped up beside me, an empty plate in her hand. I remembered seeing her at the graveside. She was the aloof blond who had stood apart from the rest of the family.

"I understand you're an old family friend," she said, a hint of mockery in her voice.

"Not really. Mostly, I'm a friend of Cinda."

"How well did you know Cousin Dale?"

"Not very well."

She waited for me to elaborate, but I had no intention of letting her draw me into a discussion about Dale until I knew just how closely she was connected with the family.

"That shrimp salad looks good, doesn't it?" I said. I scooped up a ladylike portion and offered her the serving spoon. She shook her head and made another attempt to question me as I moved on to the casserole section.

"Have you known Cinda a long time?"

"Long enough to be good friends, but I've never met any of her relatives until today. Do you live here in Walla Walla or are you from out of town?"

"Grandma and I moved to Pendleton, Oregon two years ago. The climate in this town didn't agree with Grandma." She glanced pointedly about the room, her eyes focusing briefly on the few visitors who had stopped by to comfort the family. "You could say the climate's not agreeable to a lot of people in this town."

Cinda came toward us, smiling. "I see you two have become acquainted. Did Vivian tell you we grew up together? She lived only two blocks from here."

"How nice," I said, wondering if I were speaking the truth. Vivian was two or three inches taller than Cinda, her hair artificially lightened and worn in a long sweeping bob, her slim figure expensively clad in a pale green designer suit of sheer woolen knit. She was stunning to look at, but none of her elegant camouflage managed to conceal the spiteful glint in her eyes.

Cinda moved closer to Vivian and said in a hushed voice, "I'm supposed to tell you Aunt Lydia wants you to bring her a small portion of fruit salad and two chocolate petit fours. I offered to get them for her, but she said she wanted you to bring them."

Vivian sighed, glanced resignedly at the ceiling and set down the plate she had been filling. She picked up an empty plate, plopped a small dab of fruit salad on it and crossed over to the sideboard where the pastries were laid out.

"Bring your plate," Cinda whispered to me. "We can go back to the library where we can have some privacy."

"All right, but what about you? Have you had anything to eat?"

"No, but I'm not hungry."

"Why don't you fill a plate while I pour us some coffee? Then we can have lunch together." I turned and walked over to the coffee maker before she had time to protest.

On the opposite side of the room, a telephone began to ring. A gray-haired woman in an apron stepped out of the kitchen and answered it. After a brief exchange, she set the receiver down and beckoned to Cinda.

"Please, I don't want to talk to anyone right now. Would you mind asking if I can call back later."

"It's your mother."

"Oh." Cinda set her plate down on the table and walked slowly over to the telephone. She stood beside the telephone table, resting her hand on the receiver. With an inaudible sigh, she raised it to her ear.

"Yes, Mother?" She listened silently for few moments, a frown on her face. "I'm sorry to hear that," she said. "Do you want me to come?" She listened intently to a lengthly reply.

"All right, I'll wait to hear from you, then. Tell

Grandpa I'm thinking of him." She listened a few minutes longer.

"It went all right. Look, Mom, I'd better go. I have people here and . . ."

"No, that's all right. I can take care of that." She clenched the receiver tightly and closed her eyes as though in pain.

"Yes, she's here. Do you want to speak to her?"

"All right then, I'll tell her you asked about her." She replaced the receiver, but as soon she started to pick up her plate, Great Aunt Lydia called to her from the living room.

"Come here, Cinda, I want to talk to you."

"I was afraid of that," Cinda muttered. "Come with me, will you? As soon as I find out what she wants, we can shut ourselves up in the library."

I put our plates and coffees on a small tray and followed her across the room. Vivian was hovering near her grandmother's chair, a 'cat-licked-the-cream' expression on her face.

"Was that Alene on the telephone?" Lydia asked, the pupils of her sunken eyes appearing abnormally bright. She had thrown off the afghan and was now sitting upright in her chair.

"Yes, it was. She asked about you and wanted me to give you her love."

"Hmph! Lot of good that does. What was her excuse this time? Why wasn't she here?"

"Grandpa's sick. She's been taking care of him."

"Is he dying?"

"No, it's the flu, I think, but . . ."

"Well, if he isn't dying, that new wife of his oughta be able to take care of him. Why does your mother need to be there?"

"Aunt Lydia, I'd rather not talk about this right now."

"Hmph! Aren't you forgetting something? We buried that woman's husband this morning."

"I know, Aunt Lydia, but . . ."

"It was your mother's duty to be here."

Cinda stiffened. She bent down and whispered fiercely to the old woman. "Don't you think I know that? What do you expect of me, Aunt Lydia? You of all people should know I can't make my mother do anything she doesn't want to." Cinda glanced back and saw me standing there with a tray in my hands.

"Aunt Lydia, you'll have to excuse me. Julie and I haven't had anything to eat." Motioning me to follow, she headed down the hallway.

"This was Dad's library," she said, opening a door into a dark-paneled room. Full-length draperies were drawn across the windows, making the interior seem gloomy. Kindling wood, with an under-layer of crumpled paper, had been stacked on the fireplace grate, but no one had touched a match to it and the room was cold.

As I peered around for a place to set down the tray, Cinda quietly closed the door . . . and burst into tears.

Chapter Twenty

"I'm sorry." Cinda balled up the tissues she'd used to mop up her face and threw them into the wastebasket. Her eyes and nose were red, but otherwise she appeared to be completely relaxed.

"Usually, I don't let anything Aunt Lydia says make me upset, but today was too much. I hate it when she uses me as a way to get back at my mother."

"It must be rough, being caught in the middle like that," I said. "Has there always been tension between them?"

"Always. Lydia's resentment of my mother is almost irrational. It seems to have become worse since my Grandmother Wyatt died. In a way, I can understand her jealousy. When Lydia was seventeen, she eloped with a big handsome man several years older than she was. Ralph Lahrman was a charming person, but he had little education and his talents were few. He worked hard to make a living, but his paycheck from his maintenance job was spread pretty thin once Lydia started having one baby after another.

"Pardon me, but did you say Ralph Lahrman? Was he your father's brother?"

"Oh, no. Ralph was his uncle."

"Sorry, I interrupted. Please go on with your story."

"Oh, that's all right; I can see why it puzzled you. Let's see, where was I?"

"You were talking about why Lydia was jealous of your Grandmother."

"Yes, my Grandmother Wyatt married into wealth. Her doting husband gave her anything she wanted: fashionable clothes, jewelry, sleek new cars and a beautiful home.

"When they were girls, Lydia and my grandmother were good friends, but as the contrast in their lifestyles grew more pronounced, Lydia's fragile ego couldn't hold up under it. After Grandmother died, Lydia switched the focus of her envy to my mother.

"Grandfather Wyatt had always given my mother a generous monthly allowance when she was a girl and even after Mother and Daddy were married, Grandfather kept on sending it to her. Grandpa said the money came from dividends on company stock he'd purchased in her name when she was baby. He said she was entitled to every cent of the profits."

"How did your father feel about that?"

"Not good. He wanted her to live on his income and put the money from Grandpa into a trust fund for me. My mother didn't agree. She said it was her money and she'd spend it anyway she liked. That was the only thing I ever heard them quarrel about, but I'm sure they loved each other. And me."

Cinda was sitting in a swivel chair in front of a leather-topped desk. A brass lamp sat on the left side of the desk and on the right were three silver-framed pictures. Two were of Cinda, one as a sweet-faced toddler, the other, a shy and pretty teenager in a blue prom gown. The remaining frame held the photograph of a radiant young woman in a white lace dress and veil. Standing close beside her was a man in a black tuxedo. The man was Dale Lahrman.

"Was this your parent's wedding picture?"

"Yes," she said, touching it gently with her fingers.

"Your mother is lovely, such beautiful dark eyes."

"Yes." A wistful smile lifted the corners of her lips. "Daddy loved her so much, and she was absolutely devoted to him."

"But she never visited him in prison, did she?"

Cinda stared at me, her lips stiff with displeasure. Apparently, she didn't like for me to delve too deeply into the personal lives of her parents. I thought she wasn't going to answer me, but she did.

"No, Daddy didn't want her to. He didn't want me to go see him either, but I went anyway. At first, he refused to see me, but one day he relented, hoping to convince me not to come again.

"'I don't like for you to see me in these surroundings,' he told me. 'Now, don't cry, honey. When I get out of here, I'm going to clear my name. You'll see. You go on home, now, and don't worry about me. I'm coping just fine in here.'"

"Did you stay away after that?"

"Of course not; he was my father. I went to see him every time I could, and I know he was glad to see me. He always liked to hear about the classes I was taking, and later on, about my job at city hall.

"But he refused to discuss anything that had even a remote connection to the reason he'd been sent to prison.

"And he never asked about my mother. Whenever I mentioned her name, he seemed to withdraw into himself and wouldn't talk to me."

I hated to probe too hard; Cinda had already been through a great deal of stress that day, but I needed to get as much information at I could. Sometimes the most innocent comment was the key to unraveling a sticky problem.

She was staring down at the desk, running her hands gently over the smooth leather surface. She appeared composed and open to answering any questions I asked, but was this a good time? I opened my handbag and closed my fingers around Gordy's manila envelope, but didn't draw it out.

"Do you feel like looking at some pictures? If you'd rather wait until another time, please say so."

She glanced up quickly. "Do they have anything to do with my father?"

"I'm not sure, but I think so." Studying her pale face, her swollen red-rimmed eyes, I hesitated. "Perhaps we'd better wait on these. It might be better if I go back to Richland and return after your relatives have gone home."

Cinda sat up straight in her chair and looked at me with steady eyes. "What are the pictures about? Who's in them?"

"The man who may have arranged for your father's death."

"Let me see."

The picture I handed to her was a newspaper clipping Marlene had enclosed with the other pictures she had given me. "His name is Josu Medina."

She looked at the ugly squat man and shuddered.

"I remember that man's trial. It took place several years ago. He was a monster, but I don't see how he could have been connected to Daddy."

"Possibly through this man." I passed her a picture of Oslo.

"I remember you showing me a picture of him while I was in Richland. Who is he?"

"Gerald Winston Oslo, a former inmate at the prison."

"I don't remember ever hearing his name before.

Why do you think he might be involved in my father's death?"

"He was seen talking to this man." I watched her closely as I passed her the picture of Oslo and the young man she'd rebuffed at the cemetery.

"That's Ken," she said instantly. "I might have known." Her voice sounded bitter.

"Ken?" I was startled. "You mean that's a picture of your boyfriend?"

"My former boyfriend. I broke it off with him a long time ago. I always thought he helped his father send mine to prison."

"His father? Are you telling me Ken is Allen Drukker's son?"

"He most certainly is. Besides that, Ken's a computer expert and wouldn't have had any trouble rigging Dad's computer to make it look like he was cheating the company. Whoever it was did a thorough job. No one believed my father was innocent, not even Grandpa."

"How about your mother?"

"I'm not sure. She seemed to believe in him at first. Later on . . . Well, I just don't know."

"I know this is hard for you, but I have just one last picture to show you and then we're done." I mentally crossed my fingers, hoping she could identify the woman standing by the white Cadillac with Ken.

"Why, that's Aunt Lydia's car!" Cinda threw me a puzzled glance. "When was this taken?"

"Late Sunday evening."

"Aunt Lydia had arrived by then, but that's not her standing by the car. It looks like . . ." Her words trailed off as she studied the woman in the picture more closely.

"Who? Someone you know?"

"I can't be sure without seeing her face, but I'm positive that's the way she was dressed when they arrived." She glanced back down at the picture and shook her head. "I just don't understand."

"Cinda, tell me. Who do you think she is?'

"My cousin, Vivian."

Chapter Twenty-One

Darkness had fallen by the time I left the Lahrman house. The streetlights were on, one of them filtering down through the branches of a large elm tree, casting eerie yellow patches over my jeep. While I was unlocking the door on the driver's side, a prickly sensation came over me. I swung around and peered up and down the street. No one was walking along the sidewalk. No one was lurking in the shadows of the nearby maple trees. So what was spooking me? Was it the memory of Cinda running along these streets in fear for her life? Perhaps. Whatever the reason, I was anxious to get back to my motel and lock myself in for the night.

As I pulled away from the curb, I saw the dim headlights of a car reflected in my rearview mirror. It trailed behind me all the way back to the motel. At the entrance,

159

I flipped on my signal lights and turned in. The car behind me slowed down and pulled up on the blind side of a camper.

I drew up as close to my room as I could, dashed inside and threw the deadbolt. I glanced about. Nothing appeared to have been disturbed. I checked over my luggage; it was just the way I had left it. Breathing more easily, I undressed and slipped into bed.

I was asleep when the telephone rang. Gordy, probably. Marlene wouldn't call me this late in the evening. I flipped on the bedside lamp and raised the telephone receiver to my ear.

"Hello?"

No answer, but I could hear the rise and fall of ragged breathing coming over the line.

"Hello? Who is this?"

A soft click; the line went dead.

Had someone made a mistake and called the wrong room? If so, why didn't he (or she) say so? I wouldn't have given another thought to it if hadn't been for the car that followed me to my motel. Earlier while getting ready for bed, I had placed my handbag on the night table to make sure my gun would be within easy reach. Now, I pulled it out and laid it on the pillow beside me. If someone was trying to scare me, he'd managed to get my attention.

But was that the only thing he had in mind? Had he purposely been checking my room to see if I was inside, perhaps with the intention of paying me a late night visit?

I slid out of bed and checked the draperies to be sure they were tightly closed. After assuring myself no one could crouch outside my window and peer in at me, I checked the bolt on my door and went back to bed, but left the lamp on. Unable to sleep, I laid there, planning my next move.

Was Allen Drukker or his son responsible for the threatening message I'd received that afternoon? And the anonymous telephone call just now? I'd seen the son at the funeral home and again at the cemetery. He appeared harmless, but it wouldn't hurt to do some checking on him. As for his father, I had only Cinda's biased opinion of him. It might be time for me to take a personal look at him.

Should I go in disguise? One of the standard pieces of equipment I kept in my jeep was a large carryall filled with wigs, various shades of face makeup, an assortment of eyeglasses and contact lenses, plus several different styles of wearing apparel.

Also I carried a nice selection of false appendages, my most recent addition an inflatable abdomen. With an oversized blouse and trousers, I could make myself into a most convincing pregnant woman.

No, a face-to-face contact with the elder Drukker might be best. How would he handle himself under a direct approach? It might be interesting to find out.

Chapter Twenty-Two

The Wyatt Construction Company was located on Railroad Avenue at the western end of town. The main building was of metal construction with large one-way windows facing the parking compound at the front. The area on each side of the building, as well as the extensive property at the rear, was enclosed by a twelve-foot chain link fence. The door marked OFFICE was at the front and accessible from the parking lot.

I climbed out of my jeep and glanced around, wondering where Gordy had been standing—or crouching—when he took the pictures of 'Deacon' Oslo and Ken Drukker. I couldn't spot a single place where he could have hidden. No trees, no shrubs, no board fence to duck behind. Maybe his only cover had been the dark of night.

As I opened the office door, a buzzer rang. A woman of about thirty with a thick mane of brown kinky hair was sitting behind the front counter, tapping on the keys of a computer. She didn't look up, but slid a glance in my direction without moving her head or lifting her fingers from the keyboard. After she'd kept me waiting just long enough to establish who was in charge, she swiveled around and greeted me, her voice dripping with artificial sweetness.

"How can I be of service?"

"I'd like to see Allen Drukker, please."

"Mr. Drukker? Do you have an appointment?

"No, but if you'll give him this," I said, sliding my business card across the counter, "I'm sure he'll want to see *me*." I stressed the last word.

She picked up my card with her thumb and forefinger, handling it as though it might soil her dainty red-tipped fingers. She gave the card a lazy glance. Her eyebrows raised slightly and she scrutinized it closely. A closed look came over her face. Slowly, insolently, she raked me up and down with her eyes.

If she expected me to shrivel up and slink away, she was disappointed. I stood silently by the counter, a calm and composed customer, patiently waiting to be served.

She wheeled around and disappeared through the door behind her. I could hear the tap-tap of her high-heeled pumps as they hit against the uncarpeted floor. A few minutes of silence, then the tap-tap-tap of her return.

"You can come in that way," she said, pointing to an opening at the end of the counter. As I stepped through, she said, "Follow me, please." She turned her back to me and sped down a short hallway. She stopped beside an open doorway and waved me in.

"I do hope you'll be brief," she said. "Mr. Drukker is a very busy man."

I gave her a cool, appraising glance. What was her problem? Was she sleeping with the boss? She looked the type.

As I stepped inside, I closed the door behind me, which was probably not what Ms. Curly-top had intended. Too bad. It wouldn't hurt her to stew a little.

Allen Drukker jumped up from behind his desk and walked around it, his hand extended toward me.

"To what do I owe this pleasure?" he asked, grasping my hand with all the enthusiasm of a politician. As he pumped my arm up and down, I studied him. He was a handsome man, that is, if you fancied six-foot-three inches of hard-packed muscle, a strong square jaw and red brush-cut hair.

And if you overlooked the probing blue eyes that held no hint of warmth.

"Please . . ." he said, motioning to a chair at the front of his desk, "make yourself comfortable."

As he went back to his swivel chair, I glanced quickly about the room. On the right, an oversized table that dominated three-quarters of the room was covered by an architect's blue print. On the left was an oak desk with a few scattered papers on top, a telephone, and a computer.

Settling myself in the captain's chair across from Drukker, I faced the glare of the uncovered window behind him. I almost laughed out loud at that overused maneuver to place a caller at a disadvantage. Maybe Drukker wasn't as smart as Cinda had led me to believe.

"I'm investigating an associate of yours," I said. "I believe he may have robbed my safe, and possibly might be involved in manslaughter."

"Oh? Who is that?"

"Gerald Oslo."

"I don't believe I . . ."

"Better known as Deacon," I said, looking him straight in the eyes. Unflustered, he met my gaze head on.

"I've heard of the man," he said. "What makes you think he's involved in something that happened in Richland?"

"He was seen near my office just before my safe was broken into."

"That right? Well, little lady, that's too bad. But just what does that have to do with me?"

"I thought you might have arranged it."

"Me?" He leaned back in his chair, an amused smile playing on his lips. "Now, why would I do that?"

"Perhaps to have him pick up something for you."

"I can't think of anything you might have in your possession I'd consider a threat." He grinned, showing teeth, but a guarded look had come into his eyes.

"Not even a tape with your voice on it?"

A few long seconds passed when neither of us spoke, then he leaned forward, resting his forearms on the desk in front of him.

"You're wasting my time, little lady. Speak your piece and clear the hell out of here." His face had reddened and he was peering at me as though he'd like to snap me into two with his hands.

I reached into my handbag and drew out the picture of Ken and Deacon standing outside the Wyatt Construction office; I laid it down before him. He glanced down at it, then over at me.

"So?"

"Care to comment on that scene?"

"Why should I? You seem to be the little girl with all the answers."

I scooped up the picture and dropped it back into my handbag.

"Breaking into my safe was a waste of time," I said. "Two other copies of that tape are floating around." Without waiting for his reaction, I left. Let him sweat a little; he had it coming.

I walked back to the reception area, holding my gait to a casual pace until I cleared the outer doorway, then I ran across the tarmac to my jeep.

I jumped in and shot out to the main road, hoping I'd timed things right. Gordy had told me Ken Drukker regularly spent his lunch hour at a tavern on East Isaacs

Avenue. It was now nearly noon and the time he generally showed up.

When I pulled into the parking lot, two off-white colored cars were parked among the vehicles out in front of Harry's Bar and Grill. I drove toward them for a closer inspection, wondering if one of them was the cream-colored coupe Ken had driven to the Lahrman funeral. I checked the license plate of the first car. No, that wasn't the one. I passed on to the second one, not that one either.

I drove on past, looking for an empty slot to park in. As I passed behind a SUV, I spotted a glimpse of shiny green ahead. I pulled up in back of it and read the back plate. Bingo! Gordy had been right. Ken's pickup was a beauty, far outclassing any other vehicle in front of the tavern. It was a metallic green with distinctive black and white racing stripes, tinted windows, lots of chrome, and sat gleaming in the sunlight from a fresh wash-and-dry job, the mud flaps as pristine as though they had come straight from the factory.

I parked and went inside. As my eyes adjusted to the murky interior of the tavern, I spotted Ken sitting in a booth near the rear. He was alone, nursing a beer. I wondered about that beer. Ken was an administrator in the local Public School System. Would they allow him that kind of freedom during working hours? The discouraged slump of his shoulders caused me to wonder if he even cared what they thought. Maybe he didn't care much about anything anymore.

I slid into the bench seat across from him.

"I'm a friend of Cinda's. Do you mind if I talk to you?"

"Did she send you?"

"I slid a piece of paper over in front of him, the warning note that had been left at the motel office for me. "Did you write that?" He read it slowly as though he'd never seen it before.

"So, what if I did?"

"Why?"

"Because you're not welcome in this town."

"Why not?"

"Cinda's had enough trouble; leave her alone."

"I'm trying to find out who murdered her father."

"Who says he was murdered?"

"Who says he wasn't?" He didn't respond, didn't even look at me, just picked up his mug of beer and drank.

I retrieved the warning note from the table and replaced it with the picture of him and Deacon Oslo. He gave the picture a bored glance, then eyed it sharply. I slapped another picture down beside it, the one of him and Vivian. A slow flush spread over his face and neck; a bead of perspiration appeared above his upper lip.

"Do you want to see more?" I asked.

"Who took these? You?" He spoke in a ragged whisper, his gaze glued on the pictures.

I hadn't known what kind of response to expect from him, maybe derision or angry threats, but in no way was I prepared for a man consumed by fear. You could almost see it oozing out of his pores.

"Ken . . ." I spoke slowly, trying to feel my way. "Cinda wants to know the truth and I'm trying to help her. If you have any relevant information, won't you, please, share it with me?"

At that inopportune moment, a server stopped beside Ken and plopped down a luncheon basket containing a sandwich and fries. The server pulled out his pad and addressed me.

"Are you ready to order?"

I started to shake my head, but the smell of Ken's cheeseburger had worked on my taste buds. "Please, bring me the same thing you brought him."

"Beer, too?"

"No, a diet coke, please."

As soon as the server was out of earshot, Ken laid his arm out across the table, leaned forward and spoke in a hushed voice.

"If you really are a friend of Cinda's, please don't get involved in a situation you don't understand. Cinda could get hurt in a way you never could imagine."

"Are you threatening her?"

"No! I would never do anything to hurt Cinda. Never."

"Why should I take your word for that? You've been consorting with an ex con." With my forefinger, I tapped the photo of him and Deacon.

"It's not what you think," he said. "I had a good reason."

"I'm listening."

"I can't tell you." He looked so miserable, I felt sorry for him, but so far, he hadn't given me any worthwhile information. I spent the next ten minutes trying to get him to open up; it was useless. What was making him so frightened? And how did it affect Cinda?

The server appeared with my lunch basket. While he was setting it down in front of me, Ken slid out of his side of the booth. He didn't say anything to me, didn't even look in my direction as he dropped a tip on the table and headed for the door.

I dug into my cheeseburger, wondering what my next move should be. I was certain of one thing: I'd lit a couple of fires in the Drukker camp that morning and someone was going to get burned. I hoped it wouldn't be me.

Chapter Twenty-Three

I dipped my last French fry into a blob of catsup and pushed the empty basket away. Leaning my elbows on the tabletop, I mulled over the small bits of information I'd picked up from the Drukker men. I'd shaken them up some, but not enough to provoke the kind of answers I wanted. True, both of them had exhibited signs of being worried about something they didn't want made public, but I still didn't know who had beaten up Cinda's father. Or if either one of them was responsible for the death of my dad.

It might be time for a sequel. Two Drukkers had been tapped. Why not make it three?

I left the tavern, headed back up Isaacs Avenue and took a left on Howard. When I came to the street on which the Drukkers lived, I slowed down and looked for the house number Gordy had given me. All the houses in that section of town were mansions, even if they weren't, a poor peasant like me couldn't tell the difference.

The two-and-a half story Drukker residence sat back from the street on a green acre of weedless grass. The rear end of the property was shielded from public view by a tall evergreen hedge and a scattering of maple trees, now in full leaf.

I pulled into the circular driveway and walked up three shallow brick-lined steps to a double door of smooth, polished walnut. Not a fingerprint marred the shiny surface of the solid brass door handles, and the fan-shaped window above sparkled as though it had been washed in dew. Either a bevy of house cleaners kept the place in A-1 condition or Mrs. Drukker was a fanatical housekeeper. *Would she be at home? Or was she out with her lady-friends playing bridge at the local country club?*

I pressed the doorbell and heard the faint echo of chimes from within. As I stood waiting, low static erupted from a speaker box on the right side of the doorbell. The static cleared and a warm resonant voice spoke to me.

"Please, wait. I'll be right with you." Despite this as-surance, it was quite some time before I heard the click of the deadbolt, and another few seconds before one of the vertical doors was drawn back.

"I'm sorry to have kept you waiting so long. I was out working in my rose garden."

I looked down at a dark-haired woman of about fifty, wearing a blue smock with traces of dirt on her right sleeve. She was sitting in a motorized wheelchair, a rack of garden tools hanging from one of the arm-rests. She looked up at me, a smile warming her round pretty face.

"I don't believe I know you," she said. "Should I?"

"Not until now." Returning her smile, I offered her my card. "I'm checking out a man who may have been involved in a robbery last Saturday."

She studied my card. "You're from Richland?"

"That's right."

"I don't understand. Why would you want to talk to me about something that happened sixty miles from here?

"Does the name Deacon Oslo mean anything to you?" I watched her closely for a reaction.

"Oslo? No, should it?" A slight puzzlement showed on her face, nothing more.

"He works for your husband."

"Oh, dear me, child, I wouldn't know anything about my husband's employees. You'd have to talk to him about that. Allen makes it a rule never to let his business affairs interfere with our home-life. He doesn't want to worry me, you see."

Mrs. Drukker was plainly dressed, baggy gray trousers covering her legs, and blue canvas shoes covering her feet. Her only pieces of jewelry were the simple gold wedding band on her left hand and a handsome gold chain around her neck. An emblem of some kind was attached to the chain, but it hung down inside the buttoned portion of her smock and only a small part of the top was visible.

She shifted in her chair and the emblem swung sideways on its chain, slipping free of the neckline. Wide-eyed, I stared at it, barely suppressing a gasp. I covered my near blunder with a comment.

"How very beautiful."

"Yes, isn't it a dear?" Mrs. Drukker lifted up the dangling gold emblem, a skillfully crafted pair of praying hands, and cradled it in her palm. "I wear it all the time," she said caressing it with her fingertips. "My son, Kenny, gave it to me after my auto accident. It's been such a comfort to me."

"Your accident . . . was it recent?"

"No, it happened two years ago."

"Miss Ferguson, I think we've talked long enough. I really can't help you with your investigation, and if you don't mind, I'd like to get back to my garden." She smiled to take away the sting of her words.

As I drove away, I had a hunch she knew a lot more of her husband's business affairs than she was letting on. She was a lot sharper than I'd first thought.

As I pulled up in front of the Lahrman house, Cinda opened the door to let me inside. She was looking better. If she had wept during the night, any trace of it was now concealed under a careful application of peach-tinted makeup.

"Would you like something to eat?" she asked. "We

just this minute got up from the table, so I haven't put any of the food away, yet."

"No thanks, I've already had lunch, but if you have some leftover coffee, I'm dying for a cup."

Cinda took two clean cups from the sideboard and filled them from a sterling silver coffeepot with a mirror-like sheen.

"I never use this when I'm alone," she said, appearing somewhat abashed, "but Aunt Lydia expects to be treated like royalty while she's here." At my spontaneous glance toward the fireplace, she added, "Vivian took her upstairs and is putting her to bed. Aunt Lydia always takes a nap right after she's had her lunch."

"Are they staying here for awhile?"

"I don't know; I hope not too long. I need some time to myself."

"Yes, I can understand how you would." I drained my coffee cup and set it back on the saucer. "Thanks. That hit the spot."

Like the perfect hostess she was, Cinda immediately picked up the coffeepot and made a motion toward my cup, but I smiled and waved it away.

"Cinda, I've been wondering about that picture Gordon Miller took of Vivian and Ken. Do you have any idea why they were out together on the night she came to town?"

"No . . ." She picked up her spoon and absently, needlessly, stirred her coffee around and around.

"Unless . . . Well, there was a time when Vivian had

a thing about Ken. Nearly every time his car was parked in front of our house, she made some excuse to drop in, pretending she didn't know we had company. She always came onto Ken like crazy, batting her false eyelashes at him and swishing her fanny around. Ken never did a thing to encourage her; he said she wasn't his type." She pulled her spoon out of her cup and gazed over at me.

"I suppose they could have started dating each other after we broke up, but if so, I never heard about it."

"Vivian once lived in this neighborhood, didn't she?"

"Her grandparents—that would be Great Aunt Lydia and Uncle Ralph—lived only a few blocks from here. Vivian used to visit them quite often, then after Uncle Ralph died, Vivian moved in full time with Aunt Lydia."

"Do you think she did that, hoping to see more of Ken?"

"No, I don't think that was the main reason. What I heard was Aunt Lydia wanted a companion and Vivian was happy to leave home. She didn't get along very well with her sisters."

"Is that the reason they moved away from Walla Walla?"

"No, it was for a totally different reason. About two years ago, Vivian told me Aunt Lydia had inherited a great deal of money from a distant relative. Also, a big beautiful house in Pendleton, Oregon. The two of them packed up and left here almost overnight. I didn't think much about it at the time, but later on I began to wonder about it. It wasn't in Aunt Lydia's nature to have lived so close to us all those years without bragging to my mother about any wealthy relatives she might have had."

"Have you said anything to Vivian about that picture I showed you?"

"No, did you want me to?"

"Not necessarily, but I'd be interested in her reaction. Would you mind if I talked to her alone?"

"No, not all, but why? Surely, you don't think she had anything to do with Daddy's death."

"His death? Perhaps, but I doubt it. My feeling is she might know more about the circumstances surrounding Mayor Ames's death than she's ever let on."

Cinda threw me a startled glance. "Vivian! Why, Vivian's my cousin. She would tell me if . . ." Her voice broke off as we heard light footsteps on the staircase. She leaned over and whispered to me, "Here she comes, now."

As the blond woman swaggered across the living room toward us, Cinda pushed back her chair. "Would you like to sit down and have a cup of coffee, Vivian? Julie has offered to keep you company while I put the food away."

Cinda set an unused cup and saucer down on the table and gathered up a bowl containing the remains of a fruit salad and a platter with a few sandwiches left on it. As she carried them out to the kitchen, Vivian sat down across from me.

"Well, aren't you the faithful friend," she said. "Poor little Cinda needs all she can get."

"Am I to understand you're not one of them?"

"Now, whatever gave you that idea?" She filled her cup from the coffeepot and glanced up. "I'm here, aren't I?"

My handbag was leaning against my chair. I rummaged inside it, pulled out the picture of her and Ken and passed it across the table.

"I thought there might be another reason for you to be in town," I said, watching her closely as she picked it up. A slight narrowing of her eyes was her only visible reaction.

"Nice picture of Ken," she said, her voice laced with irony.

"And the back of your head?"

"My head? What an imagination you have."

"Not according to Ken." A startled look came into her eyes. Almost instantly she ducked her head. Reaching into the pocket of her designer suit, she pulled out a cigarette and lighter. After she had lit up, she drew in a mouthful of smoke and blew a long stream of it in my direction.

"Who are you?" she asked. "And don't give me that tripe about being little Cinda's true blue friend. Or more to the point, what are you? Some nosy reporter?"

"No, I'm not a newsman. I'm an investigator, looking into Dale Lahrman's death and the circumstances leading up to it. Tell me, Vivian, do you believe he was guilty of fraud?"

I winced as she tapped her cigarette on the top of her

porcelain cup, scattering ashes on the white linen table-cloth. She sucked in again on her cigarette and blew out another stream of smoke in my direction.

"He was guilty all right and everyone knew it."

"What makes you so sure?"

"That wife of his spent money like water and the poor guy was up to his ears in debt. No wonder he started taking kickbacks; his wife pushed him into it. She's the one who ought to have been sent to prison."

"Is that what Ken thinks?"

"How should I know what Ken thinks?"

"You met with him Sunday night, didn't you?"

"So what?"

"So what did the two of you talk about?"

"It's none of your business."

"Did you ask him for more money?"

The alarmed surprise in her eyes told me I'd hit right on target. She stubbed her cigarette out in her saucer, grinding down so hard her knuckle turned white. She stood up and leaned across the table, bracing herself on the palms of her hands.

"You think you're so clever," she said, glaring down at me, her voice shaking with anger, "but you're nothing but a snake in the grass." She spun around on her high heels and marched over to the front door.

Chapter Twenty-Four

Cinda dashed out of the kitchen with a dripping dish-cloth in her hand. "What happened? I heard the front door slam; I thought you had left."

"No, it was Vivian. She ran out to her grandmother's Caddie and took off. I'm afraid I said something that upset her."

"Oh? What'd you say?"

"I suggested the reason she met with Ken Sunday night was to ask him for money."

"Ask Ken for money! Why ever would you think that?"

"She aroused my suspicions when she dodged questions about him. And another thing, she seemed awfully smug when she talked about your parents. She accused your father of taking kickbacks to support your mother's extravagances."

180

"That's not true." Cinda sank down on a dining room chair, the wet dishcloth hanging down unnoticed between her knees. "My mother was very careful about how much she spent. She never bought anything she couldn't afford. I can understand Vivian saying spiteful things about my mother. That's aunt Lydia's fault. But I can't believe she'd accuse Daddy of taking kickbacks. I always thought both she and Aunt Lydia knew he was innocent."

"Do you want me to stop the investigation? If this is becoming too painful."

"No, Julie, please don't stop now. I want to know the truth, even if it hurts."

We talked a few minutes longer, then she looked down at the wet spots on the knees of her slacks. "I'd better take this back to the kitchen, but please, don't leave yet."

"I won't. I'll stay right here at the table while you finish cleaning up the kitchen."

I pulled out my cell phone and dialed the Travelodge. At my request, the desk clerk rang Gordy's room. When he didn't answer, I dialed his cell phone number. No answer there either. I was starting to get worried about him. He hadn't contacted me in the last twenty-four hours. I hoped he hadn't gotten himself into some kind of trouble.

"Vivian? *VIVIAN* . . . I'm calling you!" The querulous voice came from upstairs.

"Oh, dear, that's Aunt Lydia." Cinda said, hurrying

out of the kitchen. "I'd better go up and see what she wants."

Cinda was gone so long, I began to wonder if I should run upstairs and see if something was wrong with Aunt Lydia. About that time I heard the slow shuffle of feet on the staircase accompanied by the tap, tap of a cane.

Aunt Lydia, fully dressed, and supported by Cinda, appeared at the bottom of the staircase. When she saw me, the old woman's face lit up.

"Well, look who's come to see me," she said, "the pretty girl with all the kiddies."

"No, Aunt Lydia, this is Julie. You remember, Julie, my friend from Richland?"

The sly gleam in Lydia's eyes told me she had known all along who I was. That old lady was about as senile as a young fox.

Cinda helped her great-aunt across the room. Standing unnoticed behind them, I watched their slow progress. My gaze was drawn to the spindly legs of the old woman. After closely observing her next few steps, I sighed inwardly. Her tottering gait was a charade; too much action in the knees. *Or was my profession making me overly suspicious?*

"Come, sit beside me, dear," she said, settling herself into the wingback chair by the fireplace. "I want to hear all about you while Cinda is fixing me a nice cup of tea."

As Cinda hurried off to the kitchen, I pulled up an ottoman and sat down, just out of arm's reach. Aunt Lydia looked like a knee tapper to me, and I hated that.

"Now, tell me, dear, what is it you do for a living?"

"I work in an office," I said, evasively.

"That's nice, dear. I'm sure you're a very good typist.

"Now, tell me all about your boyfriend . . . you do have a boyfriend, don't you?"

"A friend, yes," I said, "but we're not romantically involved." Before she could dig any further into my personal life, I plunged in with some questions of my own.

"You used to live in Walla Walla, didn't you? On Hodson Street, wasn't it?

Ignoring me, Lydia brushed an imaginary speck of dust from the flat bosom of her black dress.

"You and Cinda's mother must have known each other quite well, living as close as you did. Were you good friends?"

The old woman's head reared back as though I'd mouthed an obscenity. "Friends with that harlot? I should say not! I'll have you know my brother, Harry, and I came from a decent God-fearing family.

"I don't mind telling you the minute I laid eyes on Alene Wyatt, I knew she was trouble. And I told Harry so. I begged him not to let Dale marry her, but no, Harry wouldn't listen. He told me it wasn't any of our business who Dale married.

"Men! Spineless, that's what they are!" Her eyes were beady-bright with anger and her voice had become loud and shrill. "Harry should have paid attention to me: I told him that woman was no good.

"And see what happened? That she-devil destroyed him!"

"Are you suggesting that she . . ."

"Child, I'm not talking about that mess at Wyatt Construction. No, she cut his heart out long before that. Flouncing around in her rich clothes, flirting with other men. And that wasn't half of it. Oh, yes, that harlot did a whole lot more than just flirt." Lydia leaned toward me and tapped me on my knee. "Let me tell you what she was up to when Dale . . ."

She cast a startled glance at the dining room. Her eyes lost their feverish intensity and she sank back into her chair. A bland smile appeared on her lips.

"Now, what were we talking about, dear? Oh yes, you were telling me about your boyfriend . . ."

Cinda came across the living room, carrying a shiny silver tray on which sat a small pot of tea, a china cup and a dainty dish of petit fours. She set the tray down on the table by her great aunt's chair and spread a white linen napkin across the old lady's lap.

Grateful for the excuse to escape, I slid off the ottoman and stood up.

"I must be going," I said, peering down at my wristwatch. "Good-bye, Aunt Lydia. I enjoyed our visit."

"Cinda, I'll call you later." I waved off her offer to see me to the door and dashed out to my car.

I drove straight to my motel, hoping to find Gordy

waiting for me. Only a few vehicles were parked about the building, none of them a blue van. I checked at the front desk for a message. No luck. Empty handed, I walked back to my room and let myself in.

I gripped the door molding, too shocked to move. The drawers of the chest had been pulled out onto the floor and emptied. My underwear now lay scattered across the carpet and my night clothes had been ripped apart and flung into a corner.

The bathroom was a tangled mess of toilet paper and towels. The mirror was streaked with lipstick and gummy with toothpaste; the rest of my toiletries had been opened and dribbled over the floor.

I stepped over to the closet. A rayon blouse drooped haphazardly from a hanger and a sweater lay in a heap on the carpet, but what sickened me was the sight of my expensive gray suit and the imported silk blouse I had worn to the funeral. The only decent set of clothes in my entire wardrobe now lay in shreds at my feet.

Was this another warning?

I searched the room carefully, looking for a pair of praying hands. None.

If not Deacon Oslo, who?

Ken Drukker? He had tried to persuade me to leave town, but that hadn't worked. Could he now be trying to scare me away?

Chapter Twenty-Five

I called the desk clerk to let him know my room had been tossed. By his cautiously worded questions, I knew he was afraid I might be planning to make trouble for the motel. He offered to send the security officer over to talk with me as soon as the man came back from his break.

"When will that be?"

"I'm not sure, but probably in the next ten or fifteen minutes. In the meantime, is there anything I can do for you? Would you like someone from housekeeping to clean up the mess?"

"Yes, I would."

A middle-aged woman in a gray uniform appeared almost immediately. I asked her if she'd seen anyone enter my room in the last hour or so. She mumbled an indistinct, "No," looking so guilty I suspected someone had given her a generous bribe to unlock my door. She was short and squat with jaws like a bulldog, which at present were stubbornly clamped shut. I tried to quiz her further, but her answer to every one of my questions was a shake of her head. I finally gave up. Maybe the security officer would find a way to pry some information out of her. I surely couldn't.

I suggested she start cleaning up the bathroom while I picked up my ravaged clothing. She nodded and went out to her pushcart for cleaning materials. Still avoiding eye contact with me, she set right to work.

After I'd gathered up all of my belongings, I packed the salvageable items into my traveling case and threw the rest into the wastebasket. A few tattered garments didn't fit inside so I stacked them up on top.

The security officer had not yet made an appearance and I was restless. Feeling the need to let off some pent-up steam, I left the housekeeper to finish up alone and did a fast-paced walk toward the center of town. About eight blocks from my motel, a home-style restaurant caught my eye and I stopped in for an early dinner.

The chicken and dumplings with natural gravy and steamed vegetables sounded tempting. After my heavy lunch I really didn't need that much food, but I recklessly ordered it anyway. I could always go on short rations tomorrow.

While waiting to be served, I mulled over the activities of the past few days. Lots of action, but the pieces didn't seem to fit together. *What role did the Spokane branch of the Wyatt family play in all of this? Maybe this might be a good time to drive up to Spokane and find out.*

Should I tell Cinda what I was planning? Or keep it to myself until my return? That might be best. Otherwise, I took the risk of having her forbid me to go.

I wondered about her relationship with her mother. Cinda claimed her parents loved each other, but if that were true why was her mother still living in Spokane after her husband had been released from prison? Was she ashamed of being the wife of an ex-con? That was a possibility. After all, she'd been pampered by her father all of her life and might not have the stamina to endure the whispers and side glances of her old friends and neighbors.

Or maybe she had a legitimate concern about the health of her aged father. An unscheduled visit to Spokane might be a good way to find out.

I checked my watch. If I left right now, I'd arrive in Spokane too late in the evening to drop in on the Wyatt household unannounced. I'd better wait until morning. Hopefully, by that time Gordy would have checked in.

After finishing the plateful of home-style chicken and dumplings, minus the big heap of mashed potatoes and gravy, which I'd virtuously avoided, I waited for a refill of coffee before I went back to the motel. The serving girl appeared with the coffeepot in one hand and a slice of homemade apple pie in the other.

"The pie comes with the dinner special," she said.

I raised my hand to wave it away, but caved in when I smelled the cinnamon and apples and saw the sprinkle of sugar baked on top of the crust.

"Thank you," I said weakly as I picked up my fork. A person could have just so much will power at a time like that.

I strolled back to my motel, hoping I'd given the maid enough time to clean up my room. When I opened the door she had already left, but had done an efficient job, leaving my room orderly and impersonal.

The telephone rang. Gordy? I dashed over to pick it up.

I was wrong.

"Julie . . ." A quavering voice spoke my name, then dissolved into heartbroken sobs. But I had recognized the source.

"Nancy, what's the matter?" As she continued to cry, I spoke more loudly, trying to break through to her. "Nancy! Please, tell me what's wrong."

"Julie . . . he's gone and I don't know what to do."

"Who's gone? Shane?"

Between sobs, I caught a few intelligible words. "Shane got his . . . his check . . . you know the one he was . . . the one he was supposed to get on his birthday?'

"I remember. That was Tuesday, right?"

"Uh huh, and he wanted to take Donny on an overnight campout to celebrate and I said he could if he brought him back this morning . . . only he didn't. He didn't bring him back ever. And Julie, I don't know where Donny is." She choked up again.

"Nance, please don't cry. I'll help you find him. Have you checked with the Davises?"

"Yes, and they said Shane told them goodbye yesterday morning before he went to the lawyer to pick up his check and they haven't heard from him since.

"Julie, don't you understand? Shane has kidnapped my baby!"

"Yes, Nance, I hear you. Now tell me, have you called the police?"

"Yes, a little while ago."

"And what did they say?"

"They said . . ." A series of quavering sobs, then, "They said they'd look into it. Oh Julie, what am I going to do? Please, please, help me."

"I'll surely try, but first I need more information. Do you know where Shane planned to go on the campout?"

"He said Hood Park."

"Did you tell the police that?"

"No, I don't think so. They just asked me a lot of questions and said they would send someone out to talk to me."

"But they haven't shown up yet?"

"No."

"I'm sure they'll be there soon. And so will I, just as soon as I can get there. But first, I'd like a little more information. Will you give me a description of Shane's camper? Tell me everything about it you can remember."

I grabbed a pad and made notes as she talked, jumping in with a question when her voice faltered. "Do you know his license plate number?"

"It wasn't a number. It was one of those special plates with letters on it that spelled out his name."

"Which one? Shane or Davis?"

"Shane."

Naturally. The name Davis was too common a name to decorate Shane's bumper.

"Oh, one more thing. How did he act when you last saw him? For instance, did he make any threats against you or Donny?"

"No, he acted happy."

"Any happier than usual?"

"Well . . . I guess so. He grinned and bounced around a lot while I was getting Donny an extra set of clothes. Shane thought he should take them along in case Donny got himself dirty and needed a change." I didn't respond to that. It sounded to me as though Shane had thoroughly laid out his plans long before he picked up his son.

"All right, Nance, now listen carefully. I'm going to leave here right away and should be home within an hour and a half. When the police come, I'd like you to tell them exactly what you told me. Will you do that?"

"Yes." She was no longer sobbing, but her voice was pitifully weak.

"And Nancy, honey, don't worry. We'll find Donny."

I hoped I was right. Shane'd had more than a day's head start and could have put a lot of miles behind him by this time.

It took me only a few minutes to check out of my room. I gassed up at a nearby gas station and hit the road. Once under way, I called Cinda to let her know I was leaving town and would get back in touch with her as soon as possible.

I also called Lee to let him know where I was headed. He offered to do some checking on his end. A good friend, Lee. You could always count on him to come through for you.

Half an hour later I saw Hood Park coming up on my right and slowed down. Shane was probably long gone by now, but it wouldn't hurt to do a little checking while I was in the vicinity. Someone might have seen him and could give me a time factor to go on.

I pulled in and drove through the area where the trucks and campers were parked.

A late model travel trailer was sitting at the far end. It must have been there for some time because it had been carefully leveled and blocks placed under the front. The car or truck that had towed it in was gone.

Although dusk was coming on, I didn't see anyone around the campground. Probably everyone was still down at the river, docking their boats or getting ready for a barbecue dinner by the shoreline.

Wait! Wasn't that a light in one of the trailer windows? Better check it out.

I circled around and approached from the other side. Drawing closer, I saw the trailer was completely dark and all the blinds drawn. *I must have been mistaken about the light. Unless . . . Someone could have turned it on and then switched it off again.*

I'd better make certain. I mounted the metal steps and knocked on the door. When no one came to the door I rapped again, waited a few more seconds then stepped down. As I started to walk away, the door opened and a gray-haired woman peered out at me. She had a round motherly-looking face, except for the tight-lipped set of her mouth.

"Did you want something?" she asked.

"Yes. I'm investigating the disappearance of a little boy. He's four years old, blond, about this tall," I said, holding my hand out waist high, "and traveling with a good-looking, sandy-haired man in a camper. I wondered if . . ."

"Haven't seen him." She started to shut the door.

"Please, would you just wait a minute. I'd like to ask you just one more question."

"What is it?"

"Did you happen to see a camper truck around here with a vanity plate that spells out the name, 'Shane?' "

"Sorry." This time she did shut the door in my face, but not soon enough. Just before she closed it, I heard a faint sob coming from the interior of the trailer.

Was it Donny? I knocked on the door again. I waited a few seconds and tried once again. No answer.

Besides breaking in, there was only one other option open to me: call the police. They had the authority to make her cooperate; I didn't. I was heading back to my jeep when I heard the door of the trailer crack open.

"Andrea, is that you?"

That voice . . .

Stunned, I wheeled around and ran back. A small portion of a pale face was visible in the twilight.

"Holly? Holly Raymond? Where's Shane?"

"I don't know." Her voice trembled as she spoke. A light came on in the room behind her, giving me my first clear look at her face. A great livid bruise covered her left cheek.

"Oh, Holly," I breathed. "Did Shane did that to you?"

She nodded, self-consciously raising her hand to cover the bruised area.

"I'm so sorry, Holly. Do you want to tell me what happened?"

"Okay," she said, in a small woebegone voice.

The woman who earlier had shut the door in my face moved into the light. "If you're a friend of Holly's, you're welcome to come in."

Holly backed up to let me enter. I stepped inside and wrapped my arms around her. "Did you and Shane have a fight?" She nodded, her lips quivering. "I'm so sorry, Holly. What made him angry enough to hit you?"

"He wanted to steal Donny away from his mother. I told him it wasn't right and he said . . ." Her face crumbled and she put her hand over her mouth. An eerie whimpering sound rose in her throat; her shoulders began to shake.

I steered her over to the built-in-couch and eased her down on the seat cushion. Sitting down beside her, I held my arm around her until she had quieted.

"We argued, and when Donny began to cry, Shane hit him . . ."

A chill went over me. "Then what happened?"

"I told Shane to stop . . . but he raised his hand to hit him again and I jumped in front of Donny and Shane hit me instead. Again and again. Her lips quivered. "Andrea, I didn't know Shane could be so mean."

"Did he drive off and leave you here?" She nodded, tears puddling in her eyes. Giving her a little pat on her hand, I said, "I'm glad you're safe, now, and he can't hurt you anymore."

Bracing myself, I finally asked the question I'd been avoiding, afraid of what she might say.

"Holly, where's Donny?"

"Oh, he went fishing with Mr. Weber."

"What! Who's Mr. Weber?"

"My husband," the older woman said. "They drove down to the dock. They should be back any time, now."

"Then Donny's all right?"

"He's fine," she said. "He was shaken up some by what happened, so Ralph thought a little fishing trip would take his mind off things."

I explained to her that the police were searching for Donny and we needed to notify them right away, but that I'd like to talk to the boy first.

Before I could ask for directions to Mr. Weber's fishing spot, a truck drove up and parked beside the trailer. An elderly man in a fishing cap and dungarees climbed out and walked around to the passenger side. He pulled the heavy door open, reached inside and swung a chubby little blond boy to the ground.

"Hello, Donny," I said, swallowing the lump in my throat. "I hear you've been fishing."

"Hi, Julie," he said, running toward me. "Me and Mr. Weber caught a fish. D'ya wanna see it?"

Chapter Twenty-Six

Donny's fish was a small-mouth bass about nine inches long. He handled it with loving care, stroking it tenderly with the flat of his hand. After I'd exclaimed over it to his satisfaction, Mr. Weber helped the proud little boy put the fish in a plastic bag to take home with him.

While Donny's attention was focused on his fish, I took the opportunity to huddle with Holly. Piecing together the different bits of information she'd picked up from her conversations with Shane, it seemed likely he'd headed south toward Arizona. This was information the police should know about.

When Mrs. Weber brought out cookies and milk for Donny and the rest of us, I excused myself and stepped outside to call Nancy.

"I found Donny," I told her, "He's fine and I'm bringing him home to you."

She let out a gasp, then dissolved into a hysterical mixture of laughter and tears. The events of the past two days were fast straining my tolerance level for weepy women.

"Nancy, he's all right," I said as patiently as I could. "Honest, he is. Hold on a sec and I'll let you talk with him." I opened the door of the trailer.

"Donny, come here and tell your mommy about your fish."

After a few animated minutes of conversation with his mother, Donny handed the now fish-enhanced phone back to me. Holding the smelly instrument away from my ear, I told Nancy when to expect us and then said, "Good-bye. We'll see you soon," firmly cutting off her stream of excited questions.

Once the line was clear, I wiped the phone thoroughly with a wet nap and called the police to let them know Donny was now safe and in my care. I also passed on the information Holly had given me about Shane's probable destination.

"That conforms with a report that just came in," the dispatcher told me. "A newsman called in with some new information about twenty minutes ago. We've already alerted the units in the Phoenix area to be on the lookout for the suspect."

Several times on the way home, I glanced into the back seat at Donny. I'd tucked him into the sleeping bag I always carried in my jeep, and he was now lying with his eyes closed, his thumb in his mouth. I wondered what was going on in his little blond head. Outwardly, he hadn't shown any signs of stress, but who knew what witnessing Shane's treatment of Holly had done to that little boy's psyche?

Holly sat quietly in the passenger seat, breathing shallowly. Since we'd pulled out of Hood Park, she'd not made a sound of complaint, yet I had a hunch she was just being brave. Earlier when she'd climbed into the jeep, I'd noticed her wince and clamp a hand across her lower chest. Thinking of how Shane had mistreated her made me seethe. What a monster. He must have struck hard to leave a mark like that on her face. What other bruises—or fractured ribs—were hidden beneath her clothes? I surely hoped the police caught up with him. An abuser like Shane deserved to be put in jail. A few days behind bars would wipe that cocky smile off his face. Just the thought of it gave me a great deal of pleasure.

When we arrived at the Brio home half an hour later, the porch light was on and all the windows were lit up. As I pulled into the driveway, the whole Brio tribe—men, women and children—streamed out through the doorway to meet us. I swung open my car door and lowered Donny to the ground. He ran to his mother, his plastic-bagged fish swinging in his hand.

"See, Mommy? See what I caught?" As Nancy knelt down to wrap her arms around him and cover his face with kisses, the rest of the family clustered excitedly around them. Aunt Sadie broke away from the rest of her relatives and swallowed me up in her warm soft arms, planting a moist kiss on my forehead and one on each cheek. The whole Brio family was inclined to be overly demonstrative, but they were the most generous and loving people I've ever known.

As soon as possible I backed away, tactfully refusing the family's invitation to come inside and help them celebrate. They had their darling little boy home again; they didn't need me.

But Holly did.

I hurried back to the jeep where she was waiting. She wasn't one of the brightest persons I'd ever met, but she was gutsy, sitting there smiling, sharing in the joy of the Brio reunion while I was certain she must be in a lot of pain.

I backed out of the driveway and headed straight for the hospital emergency room. The doctor on duty was someone I knew. Although he had patients lined up in the waiting area, I managed to get a word with him as he stepped out of a cubicle.

Soon after, Holly was taken into the treatment area. Three quarters of an hour later, she was on her way to X-ray.

My hunch had been right. In addition to some extensive bruising, Shane had fractured two of her lower ribs. The doctor on duty strapped her midriff, prescribed medicine for pain and sent her home. My home. At least for the night. After that, what?

Actually, I didn't know a thing about the girl, except for the few facts I'd overheard when she registered at the emergency desk. She named her mother as next of kin and gave an address located in a town so small I'd never heard of it. Tomorrow I would have a long chat with her. Tonight the only thing she needed to be concerned with was a bowl of soup and a peaceful night's sleep.

Two houseguests within a week, both of them females in distress. At this rate, my living space was in danger of turning into a women's hostel.

Chapter Twenty-Seven

After Holly was bedded down with one of the sleeping pills the doctor had prescribed for her, I went downstairs to the office. Pulling out the lower drawer of my desk for a footrest, I sat down for some in-depth thinking. Until Holly was feeling well enough to make other housing arrangements, I shouldn't go off and leave her by herself. That meant I was stuck here in Richland for the present and would have to post-pone my trip to Spokane for at least another day.

What a disappointment. I was looking forward to contacting the Wyatt side of the family, especially Cinda's grandfather. Not only was he the kingpin of Wyatt Construction company, but he also appeared to wield a lot of power over the other members of his family. Otherwise, why hadn't Cinda's mother attended her husband's funeral? Was she merely trying to avoid a confrontation with Great Aunt Lydia? That alone didn't seem a good enough reason to leave all the funeral preparations up to Cinda. Unless, of course, the Senior Wyatt was on his deathbed. And if he wasn't, why hadn't he also attended his son-in-law's funeral?

Was there a possibility both he and Cinda's mother actually believed Dale Lahrman was guilty of taking kick backs from the firm? If so, they might not be comfortable being around Cinda, who was completely convinced her father had been framed by Allen Drukker.

Abruptly, the telephone rang. Gordy? I snatched it up.

I was wrong. It was Lee, checking to see if I were back in town. I was ashamed of my momentary disappointment at hearing his voice instead of Gordy's. I shouldn't let myself get so wrapped up in a case that I didn't have time to talk to an old friend. I thanked Lee for tracking down the information that might lead the authorities to Shane.

"Glad to do it," he said. "I hope they nail that bastard good. In my book, he should be put out of circulation permanently.

"Julie, have you talked to Nancy? I heard Davis dumped off the kid somewhere and a woman found him."

"Yes, I got lucky."

"It was you? I might have guessed. The kid okay?"

"As far as I could tell. Shane's girlfriend was on the receiving end this time. She has a couple of broken ribs."

"Ouch! That can hurt. She okay otherwise?"

"She's badly bruised and a bit demoralized, but I think she'll be all right."

"Glad to hear it.

"Julie . . . if you're not too busy, I'd like to take you out to dinner tonight. How about it?"

"Oh, Lee, I'm sorry; I've already eaten. Besides, I'm more or less stuck here until I can arrange for Holly to rejoin her family or a friend. Will you give me a rain-check?"

"Sure, fine. Well, I guess that about wraps it up for now, doesn't it?"

Not even a moron would have missed that wide-open hint for an invitation to my apartment. *Sorry, Lee, not tonight.*

"I guess it does," I said. "But the first chance I get, I'll call you and take you up on that dinner invitation. All right?"

"Sure thing, lovely lady . . . just don't wait too long."

"I won't." After we'd signed off, Lee's last remark kept playing over in my mind. *A casual remark? Or a subtle hint?*

The telephone rang again. This time it was Nancy, telling me again how grateful she was to me for finding Donny and bringing him home.

"No one but you could have found my baby that fast," she said. "Honestly, Julie, you must have a sixth sense about such things." I didn't bother to tell her she was the one who gave me the idea where to look; it wouldn't have done any good. She was determined to make a heroine of me, so I let her run on for a few more minutes. I realized she was coming down off an emotional high and needed to ventilate.

Finally, I broke in. "Is Donny in bed?"

"Yes, and sleeping like a little angel."

"Oh, that's good. Now, I'd better let you go, so you can peek in on him again. Call me if you need me for anything."

Not five minutes passed before the phone rang again. Please . . . let it not be Nancy again.

"Julie?" Gordy, at last. His voice was muffled as though his hand were cupped around the mouthpiece. "I called your motel in Walla Walla and they said you'd checked out, so I came back home to develop some pictures I took last night. I was on my way to bring them to you, only I think someone's on my tail."

"Where are you now?"

"At Kadlec."

"The hospital! Have you been hurt?"

"No, Julie, you don't understand. When I left my house about ten minutes ago, a gray sedan fell in behind me. I remembered seeing it trailing behind me on my way home from Walla Walla, but when I turned off at Wallula Junction and speeded up I thought I'd left it behind. I'd forgotten all about it until I was on my way to your office and saw the same gray car follow me around a corner. I couldn't shake it off so I led it past the city hall, circled the block and pulled up in front of the police station. When the driver passed on by me, I shot out through the exit and drove back toward the Corrado Building and cut my lights. At first I thought I'd lost him, but then I saw him turn onto Swift, so I ducked into the hospital. Can you come and get me?"

"Sure can. What part of the hospital are you in?"

"The waiting area by the emergency desk."

"I'm on my way."

I dashed upstairs, picked up my keys, peeked in at Holly—she was sleeping—and dashed back down the stairway and out to my jeep.

When I pulled up at the curb in front of the emergency entrance, Gordy was waiting just inside the glass doors. He poked his head out, peered warily to his left and to his right, then bolted across the walkway. He jumped in beside me and slammed the car door.

"You'd better take off. He's probably looking for me."

As I drove toward Stevens Drive, I asked, "Who's 'he'?"

"I don't know, but he's driving the same four-door sedan I saw in Colfax."

"Colfax? Why were you in Colfax?

"I tailed old man Drukker there."

"Old man? You mean, Allen?"

"Yeah, that's right, the old man."

I smothered a grin, knowing Gordy would go sullen on me if he thought I was amused at the way he expressed himself. "If someone followed you all the way from Colfax, there must have been a reason."

"Yeah, you got that right. Old man Drukker met

some red-hot babe at a motel and as soon as they got inside, they started climbing all over each other. They didn't even bother to turn out the lights. The curtains weren't pulled all the way shut, so I caught them in the act. I'd taken about three shots when I saw someone spying on me, so I got out of there quick."

"Did you get a good look at the guy that was watching you?"

"Not really. He ducked back behind a car when he knew I'd made him. I'm pretty sure he was wearing a ski mask."

"And he was the one that was following you?"

"Yeah, that's right, but after I lost him at Wallula I didn't spot him again until just a few minutes ago."

"I'm real interested in those pictures," I said. "Obviously, I'm not the only one, or you wouldn't have been followed. If it's all right with you, I'll pull in behind the Red Lion Hotel and take a look at them right now."

"Sure, Julie." Gordy shifted his shoulders importantly. "I hope they crack the case for you."

"Hmm," I said, half-listening as I stopped in the turn lane and waited for the traffic to clear.

Gordy was all keyed up about the night's adventures, but despite his expectations the pictures he'd taken might turn out to be valueless. Drukker might have posted a lookout at the motel merely to protect his privacy. If so, Gordy could hand over the pictures to the man who was following him and that would be the end of it.

The thing that baffled me was why a macho guy like

Allan Drukker would drive all the way to Colfax to hop into bed with a woman. Unless that woman was very, very special. I couldn't see him going all that way just to meet Ms. Curlytop from his office.

Vivian? Could Drukker be having an affair with her? Behind her cool facade was a woman with a temper. Might she not also be a woman with unrequited passion?

I drove around to the side of the hotel and pulled into a parking slot. Taking a penlight from my handbag, I held out my palm to Gordy.

"All right, let's have a look."

He slid four 5×7 pictures out of the manila envelope and passed them over to me. The first one was a shot of Drukker and a woman in a black lace teddy standing beside the bed, their backs to the window. The next two photos showed them lying on top of the bed, their arms and legs entwined. In one of these the side of the woman's face was highlighted by the bedside lamp. I held my penlight down low, studying her face.

"Look at the next picture," Gordy said. "I blew up the face. You can see it real good."

I flipped the last picture over on top of the others and flashed my penlight down over it. I gasped.

No! It couldn't be; I had to be wrong. I ran my light slowly over the picture and studied it carefully.

"Do you know who she is?" Gordy asked, his voice lifting in surprise.

"Yes, I'm afraid I do."

Chapter Twenty-Eight

I drove up Swift Avenue and made a pass by Gordy's van. Gordy wasn't talking to me. He sat stiffly in his seat, sulking because I hadn't revealed the name of the woman who had been cuddling up with Allen Drukker. Until I reported it to the police I had a good reason to keep that information to myself, but Gordy failed to see my point of view.

I circled the block again while he peered out the window, looking for any sign of the gray sedan.

"I'll make one more pass," I said. "If you still don't see anything suspicious, I'll let you out."

He made no comment. My apparent unwillingness to confide in him had pricked his ego, and he wasn't about to let me forget it. Gordy could be a trial at times, but usually he didn't pout for long. His penchant for talking was much too powerful.

I pulled my jeep in behind his van and he climbed out. "Thanks a million, Gordy. I'll be in touch." He stomped away without a backward glance.

I turned homeward, a trifle anxious about leaving Holly alone so long. She'd had a rough day. Although she'd been almost stoical about her broken ribs, she was still upset by the shameful way Shane had treated her. I didn't want her to awaken and think I too had deserted her.

Approaching my house, I began to slow down, took one startled look at the front of the building and cruised on by.

Why was my entryway dark? The light had been on when I left and it shouldn't have burned out this soon. The bulb was a new one; I'd screwed it in just before my trip to Walla Walla.

I circled the block, peering intently back into the shadows. No strange cars and no one on the streets except a man walking his dog. Nothing the least bit suspicious that I could see. No doubt, Gordy's cloak and dagger routine had unduly affected me. Light bulbs do burn out, some of them faster than others.

Yet, no harm in being cautious. I'd cruise around the area one more time and if I still didn't spot anything that appeared suspicious, I'd head for home. This time I made a wider circle around the neighborhood, encompassing several more blocks than before. That's when I spotted a gray sedan parked back in some lilac bushes at the unlighted end of a one-story duplex. A sign on the front lawn read: HOUSE FOR RENT.

Better check it out.

I cruised on up the block and parked in front of a house with no lights on, neither inside or out. After glancing up and down the street, I crawled out of my jeep and slipped back along the sidewalk.

When I came to the duplex, I cut across the dry un-mown grass and sidled up to the gray sedan half-hidden in the clump of lilacs. The license plate holder on the back fender bore the name of a car dealer in Walla Walla. Squeezing past the bushes, I peered in through the car windows. I could make out the shadowy outlines of the car seats and the steering wheel, but nothing else. I tried the doors; they were locked.

Taking out my penlight, I shined it in through the window on the driver's side. I focused the beam on the registration-card clipped to the sun visor. The name George Owen was listed above an address in Walla Walla. Neither the name nor the address rang a bell in my mind.

Back in my jeep, I did some rapid thinking. *Was that car just a look-alike of the one Gordy had seen? Could it just be a coincidence that the license plate came from a Walla Walla car dealer?* I doubted it. Especially when there was only one set of car tracks running back over the dry grass.

Whoever it was that parked that car back in the

bushes might be the same one who turned out my entry light. Even now, he might be lying in wait for me.

Holly! What would he do to her if he caught her there alone? If she told him she didn't know where I was would he believe her? Maybe I should call the police to investigate.

No . . . Not until I made sure I had a real problem to worry about and not some fantasy I'd built up in my mind.

I started up the jeep and drove on down the street. A block from my house, I parked at the curb under the overhanging branches of a towering maple tree. I climbed out and crept along on foot, my handbag slung over my shoulder, Dad's .38 resting in the roomy side pocket.

I stepped slowly through the shadowy side-yard of a two-story house, veered to my left and followed along the outside of a wire mesh fence that separated a lush green lawn from a large vegetable garden.

Fifty feet ahead of me was the back service entrance of Brio's Bake Shop. If I continued on along the outside of the wire mesh fence I could slip into their service area and peer over the board fence that surrounded the back of my building. If anyone had broken in I should be able to spot it.

Suddenly, from the opposite side of the wire fence, a huge dark blob charged out of the shadows and rushed toward me. It hit the fence that separated us with such force one of the sustaining posts wavered outward. I reeled back, my heart pounding.

The mammoth creature clawed and pummeled the fence, jostling the weakened base of the post. Between lunges, he barked ferociously, the sound echoing out over the neighborhood.

A nearby window slammed open and a male voice shouted, "Capper, shut up; shut up right now!" The big dog whined and stopped barking, but didn't retreat an inch. He continued to paw and push against the fence, making snuffling noises directly opposite me. The fence creaked under his weight and the steel post leaned farther and farther outward. Would it give way and leave me face-to-face with that ugly slobbering creature?

I didn't move, afraid even to breathe.

After a while the dog flopped down on his side of the wire mesh, growling now and then to let me know he hadn't forgotten me.

I couldn't crouch there all night; I'd better take a chance on the fence holding up even if the dog decided to take another lunge at me. I took a cautious step forward. A low menacing growl let me know the ugly beast hadn't lost interest in me.

I moved again. The growling continued as I edged away.

One step . . . Two more steps . . .

The dog charged to his feet. Snarling, he hurled the full force of his monstrous body against the wire mesh. With a metallic screech, the wire clips tore loose from the post. One long section crashed to the ground.

By then I was running along the inside of the cedar board fence behind Brio's bakery. As I drew near the service gate to my building, I dug into my pocket for the key and thrust it into the lock. I yanked the gate open, slithered through and pulled it shut. Just as it closed behind me, a big thump hit the other side, followed by a whine, then a whimper and a few snuffling sounds.

Catching my breath, I peered about me.

Brio's bakery sat cozily swathed in the soft yellow glow of a street light.

A car drove along the street, its radio blaring. As it moved on, silence dropped down around me. Even the dog was no longer making a sound.

My building lay in darkness. Not even a glimmer of light from the lamp I always left on in my office.

I crept across the spongy bark mulch at the back of my house and ducked down under the back window of my office. When my eyes had become adjusted to the darkness, I raised my head and looked in. I saw, or maybe sensed, a movement near my desk.

My imagination?

No . . . Someone was sitting at my desk. As I watched, a penlight flicked on. The man—from the back it looked like a man—began to paw through the drawers of my desk. What was he searching for? Pictures? An audio tape?

Pulling Dad's .38 from my shoulder bag, I stole silently up the steps to the security door that led to the service porch. Sliding my key into the lock, I waited a few seconds, then slowly pushed the door inward.

Straight ahead were two inside doors, one opened directly into my office, the other into the basement. If I attempted to open my office door, the intruder might hear the noise and be waiting for me. I didn't like the odds.

Moving silently to the basement door, I unlocked it and slid inside. I dug into my shoulder bag, fished out my penlight and flicked it on. Rapidly, but quietly, I descended the stairs. Crossing over to the file room door, I stood silently listening. Still no sound from above.

I crept inside, flipped on the overhead lights and opened up one of the storage cabinets. I pulled out my gun-belt and strapped it around my waist. After fitting the .38 into the holster, I moved the ladder under the dumbwaiter shaft and let down the rope.

Hand over hand, feet trailing along below me, I began to climb. When I reached the first floor level of the shaft, I stuck out my foot and felt for the ledge. In my eagerness, I misjudged the distance. The slight scrape of my shoe against the inside of the shaft sounded as loud to my ears as the slam of a door. *Had he heard? Would he open the closet door and catch me dangling there like a duck on a string?*

Overhead, my desk chair gave off a squawk. Another squawk, then the light creak of a floorboard. He was coming . . .

Frenziedly, I began to climb, hand over hand, my heart beating wildly. A foot short of the second floor level, a light flashed below me. At the same time, running footsteps sounded in the upstairs hallway. At the top of the stairs, they stopped.

"Andrea? Is that you down there?"

Holly!

The light in the shaft vanished. Feet pounded on the lower staircase and rose rapidly upward.

Panting, my muscles screaming, I pulled myself the rest of the way up the shaft. Swinging over to the ledge, I stepped out into the exercise room. I slipped the .38 out of my holster and crossed over to the door that led into the hallway. With my free hand, I twisted the knob and pulled it back a fraction of an inch. At that instant, Holly cried out.

"Who are you? What're you doing here?"

I peered through the crack in the door and saw Holly running down the hallway, fleeing toward her bedroom.

A figure in a black jumpsuit and black stocking cap lunged from the top of the stairs and bounded after her.

Gripping my gun with both hands, I stepped out into the hallway.

"Stop, or I'll shoot!"

The jumpsuit wheeled around; a gloved hand began to snake downward toward a side pocket.

"Don't! Or you're dead." The low rasp of my voice hung in the air between us.

The hand froze. Large dark eyes fixed on me.

"I'm not armed." The voice was low and husky.

"Put your hands on your head," I said, the .38 steady in my hand.

"That's right. Now, sit down on the floor with your back against the wall. Good. Now, don't move a muscle until I tell you, do you understand?"

The silent figure nodded.

Without lessening my stance, I raised my voice and called out to Holly, now standing wide-eyed on the threshold of her bedroom.

"Dial 911," I said, "and tell them to send the police."

I glanced back at the figure on the floor and saw the dark eyes flick upward.

I swung around in a crouch, my finger on the trigger of the .38.

A tall man in black stood there, a revolver in his hand. As he tilted it down to point at my head, I aimed my gun . . .

And fired.

Chapter Twenty-Nine

When the police arrived, I slid the safety on my gun into place and handed it over to them. That's when I became unglued. My knees began to tremble and I couldn't seem to get my breath. I staggered across the hall to my bedroom and sank down in Dad's old brown leather chair. Holly followed me in and sat down on the ottoman in front of me.

"Andrea, you were s-o-o-o brave. Weren't you scared?"

"Oh, yes, I was scared. I've done lots of target practice with Dad's gun, but this was the first time I'd ever pointed it at anyone." A convulsive breath rose from deep inside my chest and came shuddering out.

It was over; we were safe from that madman, but I still couldn't stop trembling.

Holly laid her hand on my wrist, comforting at first, then tightened her grip. "Were you trying to kill him?"

"No, I was aiming at his arm; I'm glad I didn't miss. If I had, Drukker would have killed both of us. I could see it in his eyes."

As I remembered the hate-filled expression on his face as the police walked him past my door, I shivered. Even in handcuffs, he looked menacing. By then, someone had bandaged his right arm and he was holding it up with his left.

I heard snatches of a conversation going on between two men in the hallway just outside my bedroom door. One of them broke away and headed down the stairs to the first floor. The other one tapped on my doorframe.

"May I come in?" Detective Kinney poked his head in through the doorway. "I thought you'd like to know we picked up Oslo. He was hiding in some bushes a few blocks from here."

"Sure, come on in," I said. "I'm glad you caught him." Even to my ears, the bravado in my voice didn't sound convincing.

He peered at me, an appraising expression on his face. "You look wiped out," he said. "Have you anything in the house to calm you? A tranquilizer? Or some brandy?"

I shook my head. "I'll be all right," I said. "I just need a little time to unclutter my thoughts."

"How about a glass of warm milk?" He darted a questioning glance at Holly.

"I'll get it," she said, rising slowly from the ottoman with her left hand cradling her ribs.

"Oh, Holly, no, you need to lie down and rest."

"Let her get it," Kinney said, quietly. "I'd like a word with you." He watched her leave the room, gazing somberly at her face.

"That boyfriend of hers sure did a number on her face. How old is she, do you know?"

"About twenty, I think. Why?"

"If she's underage, we can charge that cowboy with transporting her across a state line."

"Has he been found, yet?"

"The Phoenix police picked him up about an hour ago."

"Good!" I had to smile, picturing Shane Davis locked away in a cell. I hoped they kept him there for a good long time. He had it coming.

Holly came in, carrying a glass of steaming milk in her hands. She'd filled it almost to the top and she was walking in slow, mincing steps so as not to spill any.

"That should help some," Kinney said. He moved toward the doorway. "I'll come back later to have a talk with each one of you."

By the time he reappeared, I'd finished my milk. Holly and I were lying on the four-poster bed, talking quietly. My shakes were gone and I felt more composed.

"Oslo has cracked already," Kinney said. "At first all he did was quote from the Bible. Now, sandwiched in between his quotations are bits and pieces about

Lahrman's death and the killing of Mayor Ames. He claims he was only a minor accomplice."

"What about Allen Drukker? Has he said anything?"

"Not a word since he demanded to see his lawyer."

"What about the woman?"

"She's not saying anything either. She wouldn't even give us her name." He rubbed his chin thoughtfully. "She passed by your door a few minutes ago. You must have seen her."

"Yes, I did." The image was still fresh in my mind. Her eyes were downcast and her long dark hair had dropped down over her cheeks, screening her face. She stumbled a bit as she came abreast of my door. The attendant with her quickly placed his hand under her elbow to steady her. For a brief moment, she lifted her head and stared in at me. Her dark eyes were lifeless and she appeared to be in a trance-like state.

Kinney lifted his eyebrows in question. "Something tells me you recognized her."

"Yes, I think I know who she is. A local photographer snapped some pictures of her and Drukker up in Colfax and showed them to me."

"And . . . ?"

I didn't immediately answer him as my mind flicked backward to a short scene in Walla Walla. Cinda and I were sitting in the Lahrman family library, looking at a photograph of her parents. Her mother was so lovely . . .

I sighed. What a terrible blow this was going to be

for Cinda, but I had no right to keep the truth from the police.

"Her name is Alene Lahrman," I said, "the wife of the man Allen Drukker swindled."

Chapter Thirty

After breakfast the next morning, I asked Holly if we could have a talk.

"Sure, Andrea." She ran her hands down the side of the cotton shirt she was wearing, smoothing it over her hips. She seemed to like the feel of it, perhaps because it was clean. I'd loaned it to her along with a pair of my jeans. When Shane had driven away in his camper, Holly's suitcase had gone along with him, leaving her nothing but the clothes she was wearing, which smelled like fish. They were now in my clothes washer, getting a sudsing.

In the light of day, with the bruise on her cheek and dark rings under her eyes from not enough sleep, Holly no longer looked like a young teenager. Which she wasn't. She told me she'd dropped out of high school in her junior year to help with the family business, a combination roadside diner and gas station in Darcy, Nevada. She'd been working behind the counter for nearly three years when Shane stopped by for gas and a slice of homemade pie. He'd stayed on for dinner and a late night stroll with her through the deserted streets of town.

When Holly reached that part in her story, she blushed. Knowing Shane Davis as well as I did, I had a feeling he'd managed to get a great deal more from Holly than a few innocent kisses in the moonlight. However he'd played it, Shane managed to charm her into running away with him, promising to show her the world. To Holly, the world was anywhere other than the little backwater town of Darcy.

"It's just awful there," she said. "The wind blows all the time and makes my skin feel all gritty. I hate that. Worst of all, there's nothing to do at night except go over to the pool hall. I never went there much, though. The men were always saying naughty things to me and making jokes when I got mad."

"What did you do in your free time?"

"When my brother didn't have some dumb ball game on, I watched TV. Most of the time, though, I just stayed in my room and read a book."

"What kind of books do you like to read?"

"Harlequin romances, mostly. They're really neat. The girl always meets a man who thinks she's nice and after awhile they fall in love and get married."

After we'd talked awhile longer, I suggested she telephone her mother and let her know where she was. Tears came into Holly's eyes.

"Andrea, I can't call her, don't you see? I sneaked out when she was asleep. She wouldn't want to talk to me; she probably hates me."

"Tell me about her, Holly. What's she like? Is she pretty?"

"Well, yes, I guess. She's old, you know, nearly forty-eight."

"Did you and she fight a lot?"

"Fight?" She looked shocked. "Mom and me never fight. Mom's nice to me; Mom's nice to everybody."

"Holly, I think you'd better call her. She's probably worried about you. Even if she doesn't want to talk to you, you owe it to her to give her a call and tell her you're all right."

"What if she hangs up on me?"

"If she does, at least you tried."

When Holly finally picked up the telephone, I crossed my fingers and left the kitchen. About twenty minutes later, she came out, her eyes filled with tears, her face aglow.

"Mom wants me to come home and talk things over," she said.

I put her on a bus for home that afternoon. Just before she climbed aboard, I gave her a big hug and promised to look her up if I was ever in Nevada.

"Oh, Andrea, that would be so neat!" she cried. I'd

told her most people called me Julie, but that name didn't seem to register with her. To her, I'd probably always be Andrea. I didn't mind.

I watched the bus drive away, Holly waving from the window. I waved back, wondering how her life would turn out. Poor kid, she was so naïve.

I climbed back into my jeep and drove to the police station. At the front desk, I gave my name and asked if Detective Kinney were in. He was.

Almost immediately he opened the door into the waiting room and ushered me back to his office.

"You're looking better today," he said, gazing across his desk at me. "Feel like talking?"

"Sure, what would you like to know?"

He led me over the events of the night before, remonstrating me only once.

"Next time don't take a chance like that," he said. "Call us immediately if you have any doubts about a potentially dangerous situation. We'd rather make a false run than ending up investigating a homicide."

I smiled sweetly at him, while bristling inside. I didn't enjoy having a lecture from him, or from anyone else.

"Anything new on Drukker?" I asked.

"He's still not talking, but I think we have him cold. Oslo is filling in dates, times and places, and naming names." He laughed, a quick harsh sound, completely unlike his usual warm throaty tone. "That fancy Seattle lawyer Drukker hired is going to have a tough time trying to refute that old ex-con's testimony."

"What about the car that was parked in the bushes next to that vacant house. Did it belong to Drukker?"

"He'd been using it, apparently for quite some time. It was registered in the name of an employee who works for Wyatt Construction, but Wyatt Construction was paying the insurance and maintenance on it. We don't know if the employee's involved in any of this or not. He claimed that although it was registered in his name, another employee in the firm was the one that used it. We're still checking her out."

"Her? Was she about my height, kinky brown hair?

"Yes . . . How did you know?"

"I had a little chat with her at Drukker's office one time. She acted as though she owned him."

"That right? You do get around, don't you?"

I smiled and changed the subject. "How about Drukker's son, Ken? How much is he mixed up in all this?"

"According to Oslo, he's not involved in either Lahrman's death or the murder of that mayor over in Walla Walla. In fact, Oslo claims the only thing young Drukker knew anything about was his father's extra marital affairs."

I shifted my eyes away from his face and fidgeted in my chair. I wanted desperately to ask him another question, but didn't know how to phrase it.

"What's bothering you, Julie?" Ross Kinney's voice had regained its usual mellow tone and I sensed he was observing me closely.

"Did Deacon Oslo mention anything about my father?"

I glanced up in time to see a flicker of uncertainty on his face. He cleared his throat, picked up a pen and toyed with it in his fingers.

"Well, did he?"

"Oslo claims your father met with Allen Drukker and accused him of setting up Dale Lahrman. Drukker denied it and warned your father to keep his nose out of affairs he knew nothing about.

"After your father left the building that night, Drukker started to worry about what your father might dig up about some of his shady business deals. He ran out and jumped into one of the company trucks and followed your father's car when he left Walla Walla. Oslo rode along with him.

"They trailed behind him for about thirty miles. Then at a curve in the road when no other cars were in sight, Drukker pulled up beside your father's car and ran him off the road."

I slumped down in my chair, suddenly drained of strength. I'd always felt Dad hadn't fallen asleep at the wheel and flipped over into the ditch as the accident report suggested. Dad was much too careful of a driver for that.

Now, finally I knew the truth, knew I'd been right all along. I should have felt relieved, buoyant. But I didn't. Instead, a great flood of grief rushed over me, almost suffocating me with pain.

"Are you all right, Julie?"

"I will be," I said. "Thanks for telling me. Is there anything else I should know?"

When he shook his head, I asked just one more question.

"Please, give me your honest opinion. Will Drukker's lawyer be able to get him off?"

"My honest opinion? Julie, I don't know. It may depend on the way the jury views Oslo. I believe he's telling the truth, but he's an odd ball. Do you know, every time he's been party to what he calls 'a transgression against God,' he sends the wronged person a religious token?"

"What kind?" I asked, suspecting I already knew.

"A small trinket shaped like praying hands. Here, I'll show you." He picked up an envelope from his desk and shook out one of the little golden hands with which I'd become so familiar.

"He gave this to me while I was questioning him." Kinney scowled down at the small golden emblem, rubbing it with the tip of his finger.

"Like I said, he's an odd ball."

Chapter Thirty-One

When I left the police station, my mind was jumping from one thought to another. It was now clear to me why Ken Drukker had been so reluctant to talk with me, also why he'd asked me to drop my investigation. "Cinda could get hurt," he'd said. Now I knew what he meant. Cinda would be crushed when the truth about her mother's affair with Allen Drukker was made public.

No wonder Dale Lahrman hadn't wanted his wife to visit him in prison. He must have known she was sleeping with the man who had put him there. How that must have enraged him. There he was, stuck away in a cell while Allen Drukker was on the outside, free to pursue any activity he wanted, including taking over the local branch of the Wyatt Construction Company. No doubt

that little deal had gone through with the full coopera-
tion of Alene Wyatt Lahrman and her father.

When all the double-dealing came to light, Cinda
was going to be badly shaken. I should drive over to
Walla Walla tomorrow and have a talk with her. Maybe
I could soften the blow a little. And if Aunt Lydia and
Cousin Vivian were still there, I might be able to hurry
their departure along.

If necessary, I could drop a hint in front of Vivian
that the person who trashed my motel room had left a
clue to her identity behind. If I'd judged Vivian right,
that would worry her plenty. The more I thought about
the incident, the more certain I felt she was the culprit.
She'd had opportunity and motive, and a woman who
wore designer clothes like she did could easily tell the
difference between my low-priced rayon blouse, which
had been left undamaged, and the one of imported silk
that had been ripped to shreds.

What a vain, vengeful woman she was. And an op-
portunist. No doubt, she'd been bleeding money out of
Ken Drukker under the threat of exposing the affair between his father and Cinda's mother.

Aunt Lydia wasn't any better. The nerve of that old
lady, coming into the Lahrman house, expecting Cinda
to wait on her like an unpaid servant. Strange that the
old lady was so willing to spend even one night under
the roof of a woman she claimed to despise. Sleeping in
one of her beds, using her linens and china, sitting in
her wing chair by the fireplace.

Unless Lydia was gloating. Certainly, the minute Vivian found out about Alene Lahrman and Allen Drukker's affair, she'd have wasted no time telling her grandmother about it. Maybe Aunt Lydia actually enjoyed taking over Alene's house, daring her to come home and face the possibility of a tongue-lashing.

I pulled up at a red traffic light on George Washington Way, only a few blocks from home. While sitting there waiting for the light to turn, I was overtaken by the feeling of something left unfinished. When the green light flashed on, I changed my mind about returning to my office. Circling back to Swift Boulevard, I followed it out to the bypass highway, cut across the intersection and drove through the cemetery gates. I parked in the center lane and walked across the grass to my father's grave. I squatted down beside it.

"I got him, Dad," I whispered.

After awhile I stood up, gazing down at his name and the little plot of thick green grass. I felt sad, nothing more. Although Dad's body was lying down there under the ground in a walnut casket, his spirit was somewhere else. And I had a hunch I knew where to find it.

I rushed back to my jeep and drove straight home. I raced up the front steps, unlocked the entry door and burst into the office. I sat down in the old swivel chair and pulled out the bottom drawer of the desk. As I put my feet up, the chair gave out a comforting squawk.

"I got him, Dad," I said again. This time it was right; I felt Dad's presence all around me. In the chair, the desk, the ancient leather couch, the pictures on the wall behind me. Memories from the past tumbled over in my mind. I'd had my share of problems growing up, but Dad had always been there when I needed him. Always.

When my mother, Andrea, abandoned us, I was seven years old. Dad was a police sergeant at the time, but he handed in his resignation and opened up the investigative agency so he could look after me. If he was working on a case that took him away from home, he sometimes had to hire a baby-sitter, but if it was a simple stake out, he took me along with him. I spent a lot of my first years, bedded down with my dolls and stuffed animals in the back of his old Dodge van. I remember cuddling up to Dad, feeling loved and wanted, as he fed me hamburgers and milkshakes at all hours of the night. Maybe it wasn't much of a way to raise a little girl, but I liked it a lot better than being left at home with an elderly woman who planted herself in front of our TV and munched on peanuts and candy bars.

During those early years, Dad and I developed a special bond I never outgrew. I missed him; I always would.

I heard the outer door open and realized I'd forgotten to lock it behind me when I ran into the office. For the first time, I noticed it had grown dark outside and the foyer light had clicked on.

Hours must have passed since I first sat down, but I still wasn't ready to let go of my memories. I didn't want to see anyone; I wished whoever was walking across the foyer would just go away.

It was Lee.

"I saw your jeep out front," he said. "I thought I'd just duck my head in and say hello." He stood in the doorway, a lopsided grin on his face, tall, gangly, and incredibly dear.

"Hi, Lee. Come on in." I switched on the desk lamp and closed the bottom drawer of my desk. "I'm glad it was you. I was afraid it was a client."

He smiled. "Have you had dinner, yet?"

"No, I haven't, have you?"

He walked over to me and looked down into my eyes. I could tell he liked what he saw. "Where would you like to go?" His voice was low and husky.

"We could go upstairs," I said. "That is, if you don't mind eating spaghetti."

A slow smile spread across his face. He wrapped his long fingers around my hand, gave it a warm squeeze and tugged me gently to my feet.

"I'd like that," he said.

I thought he would.